HER IRISH INHERITANCE

ESCAPE TO IRELAND SERIES BOOK 3

MICHELE BROUDER

Editing by Jessica Peirce

Book Cover Design and Formatting by www.madcatdesigns.net

Her Irish Inheritance

ISBN-13: 9781690768326

To God be the Glory.

For my brothers, Hank and Mark,
During our darkest hours
you always made me laugh.

CHAPTER ONE

*C*aroline Egan arrived at her desk bright and early Monday morning. She was exhausted; she'd had a restless night after having dinner with her ex. His news had left her reeling.

She no sooner set her purse and bag underneath her desk at her work space when her manager, Chris, appeared at her side, her turquoise blouse and matching earrings setting off her bright-orange hair.

"We've got a meeting at nine with Dr. Walsh and Jim Munroe over in Jim's office," Chris announced.

Caroline straightened up, her eyes widening. "We do? Why?"

Chris shook her head. "I don't know. I just got a call from Jim's secretary requesting 'our presence,'" she said with a hint of sarcasm. Chris bit her lip. "Any problems with any of your patients? Anything out of the ordinary?"

Caroline shook her head. "None that I can think of."

Chris sighed. "I hate surprises. Especially on Monday mornings."

"Yeah, me too," Caroline replied, her stomach starting to do a little twist. In the ten years she'd worked as a home-care nurse for hospice, she'd never had a meeting with the CEO. He usually remained in the administrative part of the building, away from the nurses. Mentally, she reviewed everything that had happened with her patients over the last month, and could come up with nothing that would warrant a meeting with both the CEO and the Medical Director.

She pulled out her chair and sat down at her desk. Believing that organization was the key to all things, she started in on the same routine she performed every Monday morning: first, sift through the weekend report from the on-call nurses, checking to see if any of her patients had any issues over the weekend. Then it would be the team meeting with their manager, followed by consumption of copious amounts of coffee while she rang her roster of sixteen patients, seeing how their weekends had gone, if there were any pressing problems, what supplies were needed and finally, setting up the day and time for their weekly visits. But it was difficult to focus on these tasks with the meeting looming large before her.

Despite the organized chaos, Caroline loved her job. She certainly preferred working in home care to the hospital. She didn't miss that at all. She loved the freedom of home care and most of all, she loved helping people. Dying could be a difficult and painful process. It was her job to make her patients comfortable, manage and alleviate any symptoms, and provide support to the terminally ill patient and their family. If only someone could comfort her right then and tell her that everything was going to be all right. Because things had not been all right for a long time.

After listening to the weekend report, she scribbled down notes on a steno pad, preparing for her week and deciding whom to see first, based on need.

"Are you ready?" Chris reappeared at Caroline's desk, startling her.

An uncomfortable sensation fanned out inside Caroline's

chest as her heart began to race. Quietly, she stood up from her chair and headed toward the administrative offices with her boss. She liked Chris. The other woman was well respected among her nurses.

"Were you able to get any idea as to what this is about?" Caroline asked, tentative, studying the other woman's expression and trying to get a gauge.

Her boss shook her head and gave her a reassuring smile. "No, I'm in the dark, just like you. But don't worry, it's not like you're getting fired or anything."

Caroline seriously hoped not. But she couldn't help but feel she was walking straight into an ambush.

CAROLINE RARELY VENTURED into the administrative part of the building. Once in a while, she might have to go to Human Resources to update or review annual paperwork. She took a good look around. It was different than the clinical area of the building where she worked. It had a more expensive feel with its white walls, white woodwork, and expensive art.

The door to Jim Munroe's office was wide open. Caroline noticed Dr. Walsh was already there with his ever-present travel mug of coffee with the hospice logo on the side of it. The two men were in the middle of a conversation. And they looked serious. Her heart sank. They never brought you up to head office to tell you what a great job you were doing.

Chris rapped on the door and Caroline followed her in.

Dr. Walsh turned toward them and smiled, and Caroline relaxed a bit. He was a short, fat man with a beard and mustache, whose reputation was legendary among staff and patients alike. Thirty years earlier, with a vision and determination, he'd built the county's hospice from the ground up, culminating in the move, ten years back, to the current campus, which he'd designed himself. In the beginning, he was noted for visiting patients in the middle of the night, when it seemed most crises arose. To say he was beloved among patients and in the community was an understatement. However, those who worked for him knew that he ran a tight ship. He was no pushover, and he only had one set of interests in mind: those of hospice. Above all else, this was his baby. It had cost him his marriage.

Jim Munroe smiled and extended his hand, and Caroline shook it, wary. He was a totally different animal, of a different nature than Dr. Walsh. At public events, he rallied about how the nurses were the backbone of the organization, but in private meetings with his nursing staff, he was always able to pull out some report from a hired private statistician or consultant, justifying pay freezes and explaining away the fact that their wages weren't on par with those of other nurses in the community.

"Chris, Caroline, please sit down," Jim said, motioning to a set of chairs.

Dr. Walsh nodded at her. "Caroline." He sat down in one of the chairs.

Jim sat behind his desk and smiled again, but the joviality felt forced. Caroline's heart raced, making her feel jittery. She was in trouble.

"Caroline, thank you for coming in on such short notice."

Caroline wondered if he'd known her name before this meeting, as they had never had a conversation in all the years she had worked at hospice.

"We called you in here because something has come up that is an urgent and ethical matter."

Caroline shot a glance over at her boss, who didn't look at her.

"What can you tell us about your former patient, Maeve Burke?" Dr. Walsh asked.

Caught off guard, Caroline blinked. She hadn't expected a question about a patient who had died months before. She stammered, trying to recollect the pertinent facts and at the same time reminding herself to proceed with caution. Eight years of living with an attorney would do that to you.

"Mrs. Burke was in the program for a little over a year with terminal breast cancer. She was a widow with no children. Her program was pretty straightforward. Her symptoms were in good control, and she ended up being transferred to our inpatient unit for end-of-life care as there were no caregivers in the home. According to staff here, she died a peaceful death. This would have been about four or five months ago."

That was the black and white of it. But there was more that Caroline held back. She'd become very fond of Mrs. Burke and vice versa. It hadn't been long before she became friends with the Irishwoman from County Kerry. Caroline had usually seen her on Friday afternoons, always her last patient unless Mrs. Burke had other symptoms or emergencies, in which case Caroline would stop by earlier in the week. At the end of each visit, Maeve would make a pot of tea and serve scones or brown bread, and toward the end when she was getting weaker, Caroline would make the tea and bring pastry. Mrs. Burke would tell Caroline all about her life and how she and her husband had come to America decades before, about the heartache of leaving Ireland and of having no children of their own. In turn, Caroline had talked about her disappointing relationship with her former partner, Kevin. To which Mrs. Burke would reply with a smile and a wink, "That young man doesn't appreciate what he has. We need to find you a nice Irishman."

Caroline had cried when the old woman passed away. She'd felt as if she had lost a good friend. Sometimes, patients did that to you—when your lives were converging, they got into your heart and broke it.

"Anything else?" Jim asked.

"No," Caroline said slowly. "Has there been a complaint about her care?"

Dr. Walsh spoke up. "No, of course not. Everyone here knows that you are an excellent nurse and we are lucky to have you."

Caroline looked quickly to Dr. Walsh and noticed that he seemed almost sad. Her shoulders sagged, and she leaned back in her chair.

Jim sighed heavily. "We've called you here regarding Mrs. Burke's will."

"I don't know anything about that," Caroline said, and she felt Chris's eyes on her.

So, this was what this was about. Mrs. Burke had possibly left Caroline a little gift. She'd always been trying to give her things, but Caroline had firmly refused. It was not only against hospice rules for nurses to accept gifts from patients, it was unethical as well. *Well, that's no problem*, thought Caroline. *Whatever it is, I'll just refuse it.*

"Hospice has been notified by Mrs. Burke's attorney that she left you some land in Ireland."

Caroline's mouth fell open. "What?"

"Her attorney said that Mrs. Burke owned a home with ten acres in Ireland and has willed it to you."

"Oh," Caroline said, stalling for time so she could digest the information.

"Did Mrs. Burke ever mention to you that she was leaving you something in her will?"

"No, never," Caroline said, surprised. "We never once talked about her will or anything like that."

"Did you ever hint . . ." Jim couldn't even finish the sentence. Dr. Walsh put his head down.

Caroline shifted uncomfortably in her seat. "I most certainly did not."

He tried a different tack. "Did you ever accept a gift from her?"

She thought for a moment. "She was always trying to give me little presents, but I always refused. At Christmas, though, she gave me a box of chocolates and I accepted them." Caroline wondered if she'd done wrong by accepting the gift.

"There is certainly nothing wrong in that," Dr. Walsh said quietly.

What's wrong with him? Caroline wondered. *Why is he sticking up for me and at the same time looking so defeated?* Where was the ferocious and passionate Dr. Walsh she knew?

Caroline said hurriedly, "Look, I've done nothing wrong. In fact, I'll refuse the gift." She laughed nervously. "I wouldn't even know what to do with land in Ireland."

A silence fell in the room that seemed to smother them.

She glanced at Chris, who could only shrug her shoulders, looking as lost as Caroline felt.

"Right." Jim drummed his fingers on the desk. "Unfortunately, Caroline, it is a little more complicated than that."

It was quiet among them for a moment as Caroline waited for the other shoe to drop. "Mrs. Burke has also very generously left hospice one million dollars."

This revelation left Caroline surprised and confused. She sat forward in her chair, her mouth open and her eyes wide. Surprised at the fact that the little, old, unassuming woman had had that much wealth. Confused as to why there was a problem. Hospice was a not-for-profit organization that depended on its charitable donations. They would be able to do a lot with this substantial gift of money.

He continued. "There is a provision, though. In order for hospice to receive the money, you have to take the gift of the land and ownership of it. If you refuse the gift, then the bequest to hospice becomes null and void."

Caroline sank back in her chair. Yes, it was complicated, but was it truly insurmountable? Her boss bowed her head and remained quiet. What did Chris see that she did not? She felt panicky all of the sudden.

"I'm lost here," Caroline faltered.

Dr. Walsh spoke up. "It's how it looks, Caroline. It's unethical. Mrs. Burke has been extremely generous to you and to hospice. Let me be the first to say that no one here doubts your integrity. But it wouldn't look good for hospice if one its staff nurses received such largesse."

Caroline's heart plummeted to unimaginable depths as she realized they wanted the money more than they wanted her to work for them.

She looked up to Dr. Walsh who, to his credit, was embarrassed enough to look away. Jim did not look away.

"You want me to resign, is that it?" she asked.

Nobody said anything right away, and Caroline's heart sank further. Would no one defend her? Did her ten-year career at hospice mean nothing? Apparently not.

"Resign?" Chris finally spoke up. "That's ridiculous. She's one of the best nurses I've ever worked with."

"It's unfortunate . . ." Dr. Walsh said, his voice trailing off.

"Surely you can understand the position we're in, Caroline?" Jim asked. "A bequest this large can do so much for this organization as a whole. What we would be able to do for the patients and staff alike."

So that was what the official line was going to be. Caroline was going to be sacrificed for the greater good. Despite all their good intentions, their "philosophy" and their "mission statement," at the end of the day it was a numbers game.

"Surely there must be some way around this," Chris said. "Where Caroline wouldn't have to give up her job and hospice could keep their donation."

The CEO shook his head. "On Friday, the board of directors met with our attorneys and public relations department, and the best scenario for all is if Caroline would go quietly."

Caroline gave a derisive snort. "And if I refuse to resign?"

Her question was met by silence. Even Jim had stopped smiling. What was implied was that she would be fired. Something would be blown out of proportion—or worse, fabricated—and she would lose her job with no reference. It had happened before. The powers that be had a subtle way of getting rid of the troublesome employees. Years earlier, a male nurse had tried to organize a union among the nurses, and he was gone before he could pass out flyers.

"Perhaps I'll refuse the gift of land," she ventured.

A quick look of panic spread across Jim's face, but it disappeared before it could register.

But Dr. Walsh, who had remained uncomfortably silent throughout, spoke up. "Caroline, no one is more sorry than I am at the predicament that this puts you in. But even you can understand what this bequest means to us—you're out there on the front line. You see the need on a daily basis."

"And what is this bequest to be used for?" Caroline asked, her voice shaking, fury welling up within her. Indeed, she was on the front line, but rarely on the receiving end of such generosity. "Increase in the nurses' salaries? Better patient care? Or were we thinking of spending the money on administrative bonuses and expanding the campus?"

She looked at Jim. He met her stare.

"We have plans for the bequest," he said evenly.

Caroline had to think hard and fast. This was going to be a split-second decision. From deep within, she had to summon all her reserves of courage. Breaking down and railing at the unfairness of it all would be for later when she was alone. Right now, she had to focus. Any way she looked at it, her career at hospice was over as of this moment. But she wouldn't totally capitulate to their demands. She would have some say.

She sighed. "Well, it seems as if it's already been decided for me. I will resign, but there are some conditions to my resignation."

"Such as?" Jim asked, raising an eyebrow.

"I want the nurses to benefit directly from this bequest. For starters, an increase in the nurses' salaries or a bonus or something." Leveling her gaze at Jim, she said, "And not just some lousy luncheon. Something significant."

"To be honest, Caroline, I don't know if that would be possible—" Jim said.

Dr. Walsh interrupted him. "I'll personally see to it, Caroline."

"Hold on a minute, Dr. Walsh. We can't promise anything, because it would be up to the board of directors," Jim retorted.

"Then I suggest you use all your powers of persuasion, because unless that condition is met, I won't play along," Caroline interjected. "Oh, I'll resign all right, as I see I'm finished here anyway, but I'll refuse the gift, and hospice won't get that tidy little sum of a million dollars."

Jim went pale, but Dr. Walsh spoke up. "Caroline, you have my word that the nurses will be looked after."

"That's great. Then it won't be a problem to let the nursing staff know by the end of the week of their good fortune."

"Well, I don't—" Jim started.

Dr. Walsh cut him off again. "No, that won't be a problem at all."

"I'll have my resignation on Chris's desk in the morning. But I would like the full two weeks so I can transfer the care of my patients properly."

"Of course." Jim nodded.

"And I would like a recommendation, so I can get another job," Caroline said.

"I'll write that myself," Dr. Walsh volunteered.

Chris spoke up. "I assume there'll be a generous compensation package? All her vacation and personal time paid out for the remainder of the year? As well as some form of severance pay?"

Caroline hadn't even thought of that. She was still trying to come to terms with the fact that in the space of fifteen minutes, she'd lost her job. A job she loved.

The two men looked at each other.

"Of course," Jim said with a slight nod of his head.

There was nothing more to be said. Caroline stood up from her chair and walked out the door, not interested in shaking anyone's hand. Chris followed her out, silent. As soon as the door was shut behind them, Caroline started to shake violently. Chris took her by the arm and led her to the ladies' room.

Once inside, Caroline bent over the sink and let out an angry sob. She couldn't stop shaking. She turned on the tap and splashed cold water on her face. After patting her face dry with a paper towel, Caroline looked in the mirror. Crying always made her eyes appear bluer.

"I'm sorry, Caroline," Chris murmured beside her.

"Well, that was certainly interesting." Caroline let out a burst of laughter in an effort to get herself under control. She tucked her blonde hair behind her ears.

They stood there, silent, leaning against the sink.

"I have to get out to see my patients," Caroline announced.

"Are you all right to drive?" Chris asked.

"I'm fine. Really, I am."

"Let me walk you to your car," Chris said.

"No, that won't be necessary," Caroline said. She just wanted to get out of there and be alone.

"Are you sure?" Chris asked.

"Yeah, thanks anyway," Caroline answered, and she thought

Chris looked relieved. And ghostly pale. Caroline kind of felt sorry for her.

CAROLINE WENT through the rest of the day in a fog. She skipped the morning meeting and headed out to see three patients, but she didn't have the heart to tell them she'd be leaving within two weeks. Being in her patients' homes was the only thing that took her mind off of her problems. All her cares and troubles slipped away as she focused on the person in front of her and their symptoms, if they had any.

What on earth had Maeve Burke been thinking when she decided to leave her that property in Ireland? And what was she going to do with it? But more importantly, where was she going to work now?

When she arrived home, she found Jill, her best friend since nursing school, sitting on the wraparound porch of the Victorian home she and Kevin had lovingly restored. She pushed any and all thoughts of him to the outer recesses of her mind. She'd deal with him later. As she exited her car, Jill held up a bottle of wine and smiled. "Thought you could use some moral support."

"Can I ever," Caroline agreed, her shoulders sagging. She retrieved the mail from the box and unlocked the front door. Jill followed her inside to the spacious interior with its high ceilings, large windows, and gleaming hardwood floors. Caroline leafed quickly through the mail, noting a letter with an Irish stamp on it with the return address of a solicitor.

Deciding she'd look at it later, she set it down, along with her purse, on the console table in the hall, then removed her jacket and hung it on the antique oak stand.

Jill had already gone on to the kitchen, and Caroline could

hear her opening cupboards and drawers. She joined her at the kitchen table and waited while Jill uncorked the wine.

Caroline had met Jill on their first day of clinicals in nursing school, when their knees were knocking and their hands were shaking. They'd quickly become best friends, and Caroline had been Jill's maid of honor when she married. Jill currently worked in the neonatal intensive care unit at the children's hospital. Caroline was in awe of that. Nursing sick children was a calling, one that Caroline did not possess, but the NICU was a specialty within that calling where very ill newborns were kept, some weighing as little as a pound.

"I don't talk to you for three days and all of the sudden, you're a landowner in Ireland and you've lost your job!" Jill poured wine into their glasses. She assembled a platter with cheese, crackers, olives, and grapes, and laid it out on the table. "Eat. Drink."

Jill was the opposite of Caroline in looks: petite, with dark brown eyes and hair the color of midnight, cut into a sharp bob.

Caroline sighed.

"It's not right that you had to resign," Jill said. "I mean surely their corporate lawyers could have figured out a way around this."

"Apparently not," Caroline said.

"What are you going to do about the land in Ireland?" Jill asked.

"I'm going to have to sell it," Caroline said, nibbling on a piece of cheese.

Jill's wineglass halted on its way to her mouth. She looked at Caroline. "Wow, you've already made that decision? I knew you to be decisive and organized, but this is expert level."

Caroline sipped her wine and said with a smirk, "Nope. Kevin has already made that decision for me."

Jill peered at her over the rim of her glass. "Oh no. Now what did he do?"

What hadn't he done, was more the question. How could you live with someone and love them for eight years and not know them? She'd asked herself that question many times in the year since he'd left. "I went to dinner with him last night. He said he wanted to talk about things."

Jill's eyes grew wide. "Does he want to get back together?"

Caroline picked up a grape from the platter and laughed bitterly before popping it into her mouth. "Um, no. His girlfriend is pregnant."

"I am so sorry. I thought he was the best guy," Jill said.

"Yeah, me, too," Caroline said with a sour expression.

"How do you feel about that?" Jill asked. "The girlfriend being pregnant?"

Caroline shrugged. "How am I supposed to feel? When we were together we didn't want children, and now he's moved on and is over the moon about this baby coming in a few months. They're getting married next month."

Jill reached out and laid her hand over Caroline's. "I am so sorry."

"That's not the worst of it."

"There's more?" Jill asked with a look of disbelief.

Caroline couldn't even look at her friend. Her sympathy would bring tears to Caroline's eyes, and she wasn't a crier by nature. "He wants to buy me out of my half of the house so he and his girlfriend can move in."

"What?" Jill asked, enraged. "How can you sit there so calm? I'd be a raging lunatic!"

Caroline *had* turned into a raging lunatic when he'd dropped that bomb during dinner. It was cruel. Kevin knew the house was her heart and soul. But he also knew that on her own, she would never be able to afford the mortgage. He'd been paying his half since he left. But last night he'd informed her that he would no longer be paying his half of a mortgage on a property he no longer occupied.

"The most sensible thing is for me to sell the property in Ireland, so I can buy him out," she said.

Jill lifted her glass and clinked it against Caroline's. "Here's to fighting back and having a plan." After she sipped her wine, she asked, "When are you going to Ireland?"

Caroline frowned. "I have no plans to go to Ireland. I'll just ask the attorney over there to make arrangements to sell it for me."

"You're going to sell it, sight unseen?" Jill asked.

"Yes. I mean, it's no good to me," Caroline explained. "I live three thousand miles away. I live here. What in the world would I do with property I've inherited in another country?"

"There are tons of things you could do with it," Jill said. "You could rent it out for income. You could use it for your own vacation home." She laughed and added, "And just remember who your best friend is. I'm hoping for some kind of discount."

Caroline laughed, but then said seriously, "Kevin and I put a lot of money and time into this house. I don't want to live anywhere else but here."

"I can understand your attachment to your home. It's so beautiful, I wouldn't want to leave it either," Jill said. She paused. "But, Ireland, come on!"

When Caroline didn't immediately respond, Jill said, "At least go see it first before you make a decision. It would be good for you to get away. And Ireland is supposed to be very beautiful."

"I'll think about it," Caroline said. In two weeks, she was going to have all the time in the world, so it was an option she'd have to consider.

"You know, you could get a job in the NICU if you wanted," Jill suggested.

Caroline frowned. "Um, thanks but no. Kids aren't my strong suit."

Jill laughed. "How do you know?"

"Just a feeling," Caroline replied. She thought about her lack of a maternal instinct. She was never one to go gaga over babies in strollers, or even offer to hold one. Her contact had been minimal. She hadn't felt a desire, even a slight urge to have children, even when she'd been with Kevin. She was happy by herself. Her own upbringing hadn't been stellar, and she had no wish to pass that on to someone else.

"What about going back for your nurse practitioner degree?" Jill asked. "You were always talking about going on for it in nursing school."

Caroline laughed. At one time, that had been her dream. Ten years earlier. But then she'd met Kevin and they'd bought the house, and she'd been happy at hospice. All her extra time had been spent in refurbishing the house. It was time she didn't regret.

"Why did you laugh?" Jill asked, shifting in her seat, wineglass in hand.

Caroline's eyes widened. "Because it was a dream from a long time ago. And I think that ship has sailed."

"Says you," Jill pointed out.

"It's too late to go back to school. I've been out of nursing school for fifteen years."

"So?"

"I can't go back," Caroline protested.

"Yes, you can," Jill said. "How do you feel about that dream?"

Caroline gave it a thought and raised her eyebrows. "I don't know. I'd have to think about it."

"Well, I think you should consider it," Jill said.

Caroline looked evenly at her friend. "First you tell me I should visit Ireland. Then you suggest I should go back for my nurse practitioner degree. Is it your job to come over here and fill my head with foolish notions?"

"Yes!" Jill replied. "Because it gives you more options. It shows you that your life will go on after Kevin and hospice." Jill laid a slice of cheese onto a cracker. "You'd be able to afford this place on a nurse practitioner's salary." She raised her eyebrows and looked knowingly at Caroline.

A little spark lit within Caroline as she thought about the long-ago dream she had more or less given up on. School would take two years full time to complete. But Jill was right. On a nurse practitioner's salary, she'd easily be able to afford the mortgage.

With a smile on her face, she sipped her wine, happy that she had some options. "I will think about it, I promise."

After Jill had left, Caroline paced around the kitchen and living room, picking things up that were fine where they were and cleaning things that didn't need to be cleaned.

Finally, in an effort to quell Jill's voice inside her head, the one that was filling it with ideas in the name of hopes and dreams, she booted up her laptop and began to surf the internet, looking at local colleges that offered programs in the nurse practitioner degrees. She found a notepad and pen, and jotted down websites, email addresses, and phone numbers. She hoped there was still some time to apply for the fall program. She began to feel something she hadn't felt in a long time: excitement. If she went full time, she could do agency work to get her through the two years. And she was still young—she wasn't even forty yet. There'd still be twenty more years of working. After staring at the screen for a few minutes, she took a deep breath and began emailing coordinators of nurse practitioner programs at the various colleges.

When she was finished and decided there was nothing more she could do at the moment, her mind completely shifted focus. She began to think of Ireland. She dug through the pile of mail that had arrived earlier, and pulled the solicitor's envelope from its midst. She used a letter opener to slice a slit across the top of the envelope and pulled out the document from inside. The letter informed her that she'd inherited ten acres and a dwelling in Inch, Ireland. Pressing her lips together, she typed "Inch, Ireland" into the search bar at the top of her browser page.

CHAPTER TWO

*P*atrick Kelly never tired of the view from the front window of his bungalow. Spread out before him was Inch Strand and its beach. From his position high on a hill on the Dingle Peninsula, he looked down on the roofs of houses below on the descending slope. But it was always the beach itself that took his breath away: a narrow, three-mile span of golden beach with grassy sand dunes bordering it on its left side. On the other side of the inlet was the other peninsula and Macgillicuddy's Reeks, whose usually purplish range was now shrouded in low-hanging white cloud cover.

It was going to be a good day for wind surfing. Inch Beach was located between the Iveragh and Dingle Peninsulas in the southwest of Ireland, which at times created a perfect wind trap. From his living-room window, he saw there were plenty of walkers on the beach. He preferred someone to be around if something happened. He was extra cautious. He had to be.

He finished his first cup of tea of the day and headed out. Before he left, he opened the door of the bedroom that was shared by his two daughters, Gemma, aged six, and Lucy, just gone four, who was already giving him a run for his money.

The girls were nestled in their beds, the room an explosion of pink except for Lucy's bed, which was done up in yellow. He stood in the doorway of their bedroom for a moment, smiling at the sight of them, and closed the door softly behind him. As he walked down the hall to the kitchen, he passed a framed photo taken on his wedding day. He looked at his dark-haired bride and whispered, "Good morning, love."

As he stood at the kitchen sink rinsing out his teacup, he glanced out the window. He took in the flat, golden-brown scrub of the mountain. By July, the area would be covered in fuchsia, gorse, and montbretia, which grew wild on the peninsula.

The back door opened and his sister, Deirdre, walked in.

"Girls still sleeping?" she asked in a whisper.

He nodded, turning off the tap and putting his teacup in the drying rack.

"Going windsurfing first?" she asked. His sister was two years younger than him, and they resembled each other, although his eyes were gray to her blue, and her hair retained the color of a chestnut, while life had grayed his somewhat.

"Yes, I'll get in a bit before I head off to work," he said.

Deirdre smiled. "I'll drop the girls off to Ma later in the morning. I don't have to be at the stables until noon today." Unlike him, she was an avid horseback rider, giving lessons out of her own stables.

"Thank you," he said.

"Would you stop thanking me?" she said, exasperated.

He shrugged. If it weren't for his sister and mother, he didn't know how he would have coped.

"Did you get the invitation for Marie's wedding?" Deirdre asked, referring to their cousin, who was getting married the last Saturday in June.

"I think I saw something in the pile of post that came yesterday," he said. "I haven't had a chance to open it."

"Just be careful," she warned.

He looked at her with a frown. "Why?"

"Because Ma might think it would be a good idea for you to bring someone."

"Like a plus one?" he asked, incredulous. How could his own mother even think he was ready to move on?

Patrick sighed. He couldn't remember his mother being so meddlesome when he was younger. It was like him getting remarried had become her life's work.

That was the last thing on his mind: weddings and bringing dates. He had no time or inclination for any of that.

"Gotta go," he said. With his hand on the doorknob, he turned to his sister and said, "Oh, watch Lucy with the bananas. She's on that kick now. Had three of them yesterday."

Deirdre chuckled. "Will do. Don't worry, they'll be fine."

Patrick used to love this time of day: early morning, when the day was so full of hope and promise. He drove his car slowly down the narrow, winding lane to the main road that led to the town of Dingle to the right, or back to the mainland to the left. When he came to the bottom of the hill, he noticed a rental car parked at the side of the road with its flashers on. At the side of the car stood a young couple in their mid-twenties. The man had his hands on his hips and looked up and down the main road. Patrick braked his car to a stop and rolled down the window.

"Everything all right?" he asked.

They approached his car. The woman had long black hair and her skin was dewy. They were so young. Just over forty himself, they made him feel ancient.

"We're looking for Annascaul," said the man. Patrick detected a German accent.

The young woman bent down until she was eye level with Patrick. She smiled. "We're on our honeymoon."

"Congratulations," Patrick said automatically. Parts of Patrick had been and remained on autopilot these last four years.

"We're stopping in Annascaul to see Tom Crean," the woman said. She seemed naturally chatty, her husband more reserved.

She referred to Tom Crean as if he were still living, although he'd been dead for decades. Even after all this time, they were all still proud of their Antarctic explorer. He was a legend. A man who had walked thirty-five miles in sub-freezing temperatures to save the life of another explorer. He'd done Kerry proud.

"You've passed the turnoff," Patrick told them. "Go back the way you came and you'll see the sign for Annascaul. It's not that far. A few miles."

"Tonight, we're going to drink a toast to him at his pub," the husband said, referring to Crean's bar, the South Pole Inn, which was still in operation.

Once they had their directions, they went on their way. Patrick watched them talking and laughing as they pulled back out onto the main road. Envious of them. So full of hope and unaware of what the future held. He'd been like that once. But not anymore.

Eventually, he drove down to the beach. There was a small group of walkers on the beach and the familiar black lab who was there on a regular basis, running back and forth across the sand, fetching the same tennis ball over and over again. Patrick, with his windsurfing board at his side, nodded in recognition to some of the walkers. Most of them were locals like himself and although he didn't know most of their first names, he recognized some of them. They were there almost every morning, walking. Like he was with the windsurfing. It was almost like a religion to all of them.

He would never go out on the water without someone being on the beach. Never alone. That would be too dangerous and too irresponsible. There had been a time in his life, years ago, when he would never have given that another thought. But not now. Not after all that had happened.

After he parked the car on the beach, he quickly pulled on his wetsuit. His bare feet hit the damp sand and he trotted toward the waves. There was a fair amount of wind and the surf looked good.

The water was ice cold. It always was. The island was too far north in the Atlantic for it ever to get warm. Not like the warm of the ocean around Florida. That had been like bath water when he and Maureen had gone there.

He trod through the water, finding it bracing but not minding. Once up on the board, he let the wind do the rest. He anchored himself on the board as the wind whipped up his sail and his board cut across the inlet at an angle. Seawater sprayed him and he smiled. Exhilaration flooded him and he let the rush fill him up. From his board, he took in the beach and the expanse of dunes behind it, the wind blowing through the grasses. There was the restaurant on the beach, not open yet, too early. An elderly man sat at one of the picnic tables outside with his dog, an Irish collie, beside him. Patrick turned his head and let his gaze wander up the Slieve Mish Mountains until he found the roofline of his own house. It comforted him to know that his girls were tucked sound in their beds. He liked to be alone on the water, all by himself, gliding across the Atlantic, alone with his thoughts.

After an hour, he pulled his board from the water and trotted back to his car, leaning the board up against it while he towel-dried his hair and changed back into his clothes.

Once he was finished, he headed out to work with the intention of just making it through the day. He could only take things one day at a time. Because one never knew what to expect.

CHAPTER THREE

*C*aroline stared out the window at the passing Irish scenery. She'd flown into Shannon airport earlier that morning, the first Monday in June, for a two-week stay. She'd made arrangements to stay at a B & B in Inch on the Dingle Peninsula, not far from where her inheritance was located. After she departed the airport in her rental car, she drove slowly through County Limerick, relaxing a bit once she reached the welcome sign for County Kerry. It had taken her almost two hours to get that far.

She'd expected the Dingle Peninsula to resemble the countryside Ireland was noted for, similar to what she'd just passed through: a lot of green, hilly slopes and valleys dotted with farmhouses, sheep, and cattle, as well as low stone boundary walls. But once she drove through Castlemaine and found herself on the straight run to Inch, the scenery changed. Along her left side was an inlet of the Atlantic Ocean. The houses and cottages that ran alongside it seemed to be almost at sea level. Out of her right-side window, the land was more elevated and rose into the mountain range of the Dingle Peninsula. It was a golden-brown scrubbed mountain, no evidence at all of the greenery she'd just left before she entered the peninsula. At the top, a narrow spine of the mountain range extended off into the distance. Caroline continued to drive down the road, noting only one gas station and a variety of houses: farmhouses, cottages, and more recent builds. She passed one small village that had two restaurants and that was about it. She saw the sign for Inch and slowed down. As the road ascended around the curve, she noticed a few cliffside parking spots overlooking Inch beach. She drove down the narrow lane to the beach to catch her breath.

She bypassed the little car park next to the café at Inch Beach, instead heading for the beach itself. She knew she should head straight to her B & B, but as soon as she caught sight of the beach, the grassy dunes, and the ocean, the pull was too strong to resist. Ignoring the jet lag, she stepped out of the car and took a deep breath of the salty air. Cars were parked along the beach as far as the eye could see. A bright-green camper van advertising surfing lessons was open for business and had various surfboards leaning against the outside of it. A guy in his late twenties to early thirties, with long hair pulled back in a ponytail and wearing cut-off jeans, a T-shirt, and flip flops—the owner, presumably—was engaged in conversation with a man wearing a wetsuit and holding a windsurfing board under his arm.

Caroline looked around. Whatever she had expected Inch, Ireland to be, this was not it. She'd never heard of the place before she'd received that letter from the solicitor. As she stepped onto the beach, her gaze swept in a panoramic view of the beach, ocean, and mountains. Scattered above the hill were a few houses and pastures in a patchwork quilt of greenery that ascended into a brown scrub of a mountain.

She kicked off her shoes and set her bare feet on the packed, damp sand. It was always good to be at a beach. She'd always loved it. Rare childhood outings to the shore had provided a relief and distraction from the reality of her home life. *Why do I never make time for it anymore?* she wondered.

As she walked past the caravan, she could hear snippets of the conversation between the man in the wetsuit and the owner. Bits about the wind and condition of the waves and the water. Caroline walked right past them, toward the surf, and let the Atlantic wash over her bare feet. After a few minutes of just gazing at the horizon and filling her lungs with sea air, she turned and began to walk along the shore.

Ambitious, she walked a long way, just skirting the ocean where it met the sand. The water was cold. After half an hour and feeling more relaxed, she turned and headed back to her car. It was time to find the B & B she had booked into and check in.

Back at her rental car, she brushed the sand off her feet and slipped on her shoes. Tired and yawning, she started up the car and headed toward the narrow road that led out from the beach. There was a glare from the sun, and she realized she should have put on her sunglasses. Once clear of the beach, she increased pressure on the gas pedal, just slightly. She did not see the man kneeling to tie his shoelace until the last minute. Quickly, she veered to the left to avoid hitting him and as she did, she felt the car roll over something resulting in a loud scraping and crunching noise. She cringed. What had she run over? Caroline jammed on the brakes and pulled over and parked the car.

As soon as she got out of the car, she saw the man in the wetsuit, the one who'd been conversing with the young guy at the caravan. He was a bit older than her, and his eyes were as gray as the ocean, albeit a stormy one. Her gaze traveled to behind her car and her eyes rested on a windsurfing board and its sail. Or what was left of it. The sail and pole were mangled and the board was broken.

She turned to look at the man. "Are you all right?" she asked, approaching him.

Thunder and fury darkened the man's features. "You could have killed me!" he shouted.

Caroline took a step back, flinching. "Did I hit you?" she asked, all sorts of nightmarish scenarios parading across her mind.

"No, but you almost did," he said, his voice thick with anger. "Why weren't you watching where you were going?"

"I'm so sorry, it was an accident," she said.

"Yeah, well, careless accidents can get people killed!"

"Again, I am sorry," she said. Looking around, she noticed a lot of eyes glancing in their direction.

The man surveyed the damage to his board. "You've destroyed it."

Caroline stammered, "I'll replace it. I'll pay for it."

Before she could ask for his name and address, he picked up what was left of his damaged windsurfing board and stomped off, sand flying. He glanced over his shoulder at her and said, "Damned tourists!"

"So much for Irish hospitality," Caroline shot back. He did not turn around.

Rattled, Caroline managed to climb back into the car, and before she turned on the ignition, she dug around the inside of her purse for her sunglasses, her hands shaking. Before she drove off, she took some deep breaths, trying to settle her nerves.

Of course he'd be pretty shaken up, almost having been hit, but his reaction seemed a bit over the top. Her first day in Ireland and she'd almost run someone down. The sooner she sold the property and returned to the States, the better.

THE B & B WAS A FEW MINUTES' drive from the beach. It was a long, cream-colored bungalow with big windows. A painted sign hung from a black wrought-iron post out front: *Sea View B & B*. Caroline stood at the front door before entering and turned around, taking in the commanding view of the beach she'd just left. She tried to push the angry Irishman as far as possible from her mind. The more she thought about the incident, the more it made her blood boil. She hadn't even hit him, and he had just lost it.

There were all sorts of signs next to the door. The seal of the Irish Tourist Board was the most prominent one, and there were similar medallions alongside it.

Caroline pushed through the front door, pulling her suitcase and carry-on behind her, landing in the front hall. Various potted plants were scattered around on the cream tiled floor. The walls were painted in light colors, and there was a stand of brochures of local interests next to a rattan sofa.

A woman emerged from the back of the house. She was tall, almost six foot, with red hair and a solid figure. She wiped her hands on her apron.

"I thought I heard someone come in. You're Caroline Egan?" the woman asked. "My psychic ability is due to the fact that you're the last guest I'm expecting. And you look like an American."

Caroline wondered what an American looked like but decided not to ask.

"How was your flight?" the woman asked.

"Good," Caroline answered.

"Before I show you your room, I'll just go over a few things," the woman said. "First, I'm Breda O'Halloran. Myself or my husband Joe are always around if you need anything. Joe doesn't say much, and that's okay because I do enough talking for both of us." She let out a fit of laughter which Caroline found contagious, and she found herself laughing as well, momentarily forgetting the incident at the beach.

Breda pulled herself together and continued. "Now, breakfast is served every morning between the hours of seven and ten. I'll show you where the dining room is," she said. She walked about five paces and opened a door that led to a spacious room, bright, airy, and light colored with a commanding view of the beach below. There were square tables scattered throughout the room, each surrounded by four straight-backed chairs. All the tables were covered in white linen. Caroline smiled at the sight of it. It looked very welcoming.

Breda picked up Caroline's carry-on and nodded toward her suitcase. "Does that thing have wheels on it? If not, I'll carry it for you."

"Nope, it's got wheels."

As they headed down a corridor, Breda said over her shoulder, "You can come and go as you please, obviously, but the doors are locked at midnight." She paused and turned around. "As this is also our private home, I ask that you refrain from bringing strange men overnight."

Caroline reddened. "Of course."

"Here we are," Breda sang as she opened a door. She set down the carry-on and stood for a moment in the room.

Caroline scanned the room that was going to be her home for the next two weeks. There was one double bed with a quilt on it and like the rest of the house, it was done up in light pastel colors. There was an en-suite bathroom with a skylight that held a white sink, toilet, and shower stall. On the opposite side of the bed was an oak dresser and a desk. On top of the dresser was a television, and on top of the desk was a tray that held a kettle, a bowl of sugar, a bowl of tea bags and sachets of instant coffee, and two individual packets of biscuits.

"Also, if you want a dinner here, that would be an additional supplement of ten euros," Breda added. "And, if you need any directions or anything, anything at all, don't hesitate to ask. Joe and I are here to make your stay as pleasant and comfortable as possible."

"Thank you," Caroline said. "The room is lovely."

Breda nodded proudly. "I'll leave you to get on with it."

Before she left, Caroline asked, "Can you give me directions to Dingle?" Her plan was to freshen up and rest before heading out to the solicitor's office.

"The town?"

Caroline nodded.

"When you pull out of the driveway here, you'll make a right and drive along the coast road and just follow the signs for Dingle. It's about a thirty-five, forty-minute drive from here," Breda said. "The town will be packed today, so it might be difficult to find a parking spot."

"I'll manage." Caroline smiled. Surely, the solicitor would have a parking lot with his office.

"What are you planning to see in Dingle?" Breda asked.

"Nothing right now. I need to go and meet a solicitor," Caroline replied.

"Today?" Breda asked. "Oh, he wouldn't be there today."

Caroline frowned in confusion.

Breda smiled. "It's the June bank holiday. Everything is closed today. That's why the beach is so packed. He'll be back tomorrow."

"Oh," Caroline said, not expecting this. She sighed. It was a waste of a day. If she'd known that, she would have flown in the next day. She'd even told the solicitor the date of her arrival, and his response via email had been to stop in any time.

The knowledge that she wouldn't be able to meet the solicitor as planned, combined with the jet lag and the near miss at the beach, made her feel suddenly very tired.

It would just have to wait. Unfortunately, Caroline's strong suit was not patience. Once she made a decision to do something, she didn't like to wait.

After she made herself a cup of instant coffee and added plenty of sugar and creamer to make it more palatable, she sat down on the edge of the bed and stared out the window at the beach, beginning to feel lulled.

Caroline felt slightly adrift. She had never traveled anywhere by herself before, not even in the States. She wasn't sure quite what to do, or even what she wanted to do. In the past, when she and Kevin had traveled, they'd explored everything together. But Kevin had done most of the research. Caroline would pick up a tour book from the bookstore and pick out a few must-see places on her list, but that was all. And they'd walked everywhere once they were situated in their hotel. Caroline could already see that here, walking down to the beach and the restaurant would be all that was doable. There was no boardwalk with little shops or anything like that. There was only an endless road of lonely, rugged coastline.

After she finished the watery coffee, fatigue overcame her, and she fell asleep on the bed.

CHAPTER FOUR

*P*atrick washed the dishes at the sink from their supper of beans on toast. The girls had had a proper dinner at his mother's earlier in the day. Once the ware was washed and put away, he went to the utility room off the kitchen and threw in a load of wash. He was still a bit shaken up after having almost been run down by that tourist. Deep down, he knew he'd overreacted, but he didn't care. It was enough that his daughters had lost their mother. He had to make sure they didn't end up orphans. And that woman had wrecked his windsurfing board. He'd left the pieces of the damaged board in the garage, deciding to deal with it later. It was definitely beyond repair. Now what was he going to do? The job in the housing estate in Tralee had finished on Friday, and he could afford to take off a few days, but no more than that. And certainly, he couldn't justify buying a new board. He should have taken that tourist up on her offer to replace it. But he'd been so angry he'd left before he could give her his details.

Lucy, in yellow pajamas that matched her blonde hair, appeared in the doorway, crying. She was prone to that sometimes. Just burst into tears for any reason. He knew how she felt. Sometimes he felt like crying, too.

Lifting her in his arms, he pulled her close. She laid her head on his shoulder and the crying gradually reduced to a sniffle. Exiting the room, he saw Gemma parked on the floor in front of the television. He allowed a little television before bed. The clock said it was Lucy's bedtime, and he carried her back to the room she shared with Gemma. He pulled up the covers, tucking her in.

"When's Gemma coming to bed?" she asked like she did every night.

"Soon," he replied. To distract her, he picked up one of her bedtime books. "What story will we read tonight?"

He stretched out next to her, she sat up, and he began to read in earnest, making the appropriate noises and voices, which drew giggles from Lucy.

"She doesn't sound like that!" Lucy protested, as Patrick did his best impression of a high-pitched voice for one of the female characters.

"Yes she does!" Patrick replied in mock defense.

Lucy eyed him suspiciously and laid her head on her pillow, yawning. The little girl went from dawn to dusk without a nap and by the time evening rolled around, she was more than ready for bed. Six months before, it had become nothing short of a wrestling match trying to get her to go down for her afternoon nap; she was having none of it. Finally, taking his mother's advice, he stopped trying and eliminated the naps and just put her to bed an hour earlier in the evening.

As he continued to read, he cast a sideways glance at her and noticed her eyes beginning to close. He read a little bit more before slowly getting up from the bed, careful not to wake her. Leaving only the night-light on, he tiptoed out of the room.

One down, one to go.

Gemma had migrated to the sofa and was on her side, wrapped in her pink blanket and sucking her thumb. That was a new thing, and Patrick wondered if it was something to do with her mother's death. At the suggestion of their GP, Patrick had enrolled the girl in some art therapy, which had seemed to help, but how did one tell with someone so young? It had come to the point where he couldn't help but wonder if any behavior such as a tantrum, or being too quiet, was related to Maureen's death. How did one know if it was grief or just normal childhood behavior? He knew Gemma remembered her mother, or had impressions of her, anyway. Recently, he had overheard her explaining to Lucy about their mother, pointing her out in a picture. Lucy'd had a confused look on her face. And why shouldn't she? Before she was even a day old, her mother had died.

His phone rang, distracting him from his thoughts about his broken and bereaved family. With his phone to his ear, he began the evening ritual of tidying up the sitting room, throwing everything into the toy box in the corner of the room.

"Hi, Deirdre, what's up?" He was close to his sister and was also grateful that she wasn't one to hover. She was there if he needed her but wasn't intrusive.

"I have some news and a forewarning," she started.

He laughed. "Forewarning" was their code word for their mother's desire to run their lives. He didn't know how Deirdre survived still living at home.

"Give it to me straight," he said.

"There's a rumor going around that an American has inherited the Burke homeplace," she started.

Patrick groaned. The rumors had started once the news of Maeve's death had reached them months ago. Everyone wondered who had been left the property. Maeve had no descendants, and the rest of her family had died out.

But that wasn't what annoyed him. His mother would be all over this, and she could possibly make his life not worth living.

"Let me guess," Patrick said. "Ma wants me to buy the Burke place and marry Edel?" The Burke place was a plot of land around which the Kelly land horseshoed, along with the other neighbor, the Fitzgibbons. His mother had it in her mind that Patrick should marry the Fitzgibbon girl, Edel, to join the two farms, and now if the Burke place were to go on the market, she'd push him to buy it if she didn't buy it herself. But he had no interest in purchasing the Burke place or in marrying Edel. Edel was a nice girl who didn't really hide the fact that she had a crush on him. It had long been her dream—and his mother's— that they would marry. Even before he had married Maureen. But he wasn't going to marry just anyone for the sake of wrapping things up in a nice, tidy bow. He wasn't too keen on ever getting married again. He couldn't go through that kind of pain and trauma again.

Deirdre laughed. "She can't understand why you don't like Edel."

"I like her. I also like the postman, but I don't want to marry him," he said.

"Like I said, just giving you a heads-up," Deirdre said.

"Thanks. Any word on who this person is who's inherited the property?" he asked, not that it had any bearing on his life, even if his mother thought it did. His mother's argument was that Edel would be the solution to his problems. As if there was a solution to grief or the loss of one's wife.

He knew the list by heart. They'd known Edel all their lives. They knew the family. The land could be made into one big farm. She'd be a good mother to the girls. As many times as he explained it to his mother, she refused to see it. It would be no good for anyone if he were to marry someone he didn't love just for the sake of the girls. That would actually be the worst thing he could do.

"No, some American, that's all I know," Deirdre said. "I wonder if he'll show up or just hang a 'for sale' sign out front."

"Who knows?" he replied.

"It's prime location. It would fetch a good price," Deirdre said.

"I'm curious to see if they sell it or will they hang onto it," he said, wondering how anyone could not be enchanted by the surrounding scenery of Inch.

"Did you want to go windsurfing in the morning?" Deirdre asked.

"I can't. My board got busted up at the beach," he explained.

"How did that happen?"

"Some careless eejit ran over it with her rental car," he said, frustrated.

"You'll have to replace it," Deirdre said.

He nodded. "I'll pick up a used board for the time being." Windsurfing was his way of relaxing. Coping. Dealing with stress.

"Are you and the girls coming for dinner tomorrow?"

"Since I'm not working, we might as well."

"Do you want company tonight?" she asked.

In the beginning, after Maureen's death, Deirdre had been there all the time, helping with the girls, especially Lucy, who was just an infant at the time. And in the evening when the girls were asleep, he'd sometimes cried on his sister's shoulder. But after four years, that need had become less and less. Slowly, he was moving on.

"Nah, I'm good. Knackered actually. I'm going to have an early night."

Once Gemma was in bed, he went out to the garage, leaving the door open so he could hear if one of the girls woke up. He sat on the bench and began lifting weights, liking the feel of the burn in his muscles.

After a shower, he grabbed a bottle of beer and twisted the cap off. He cranked open the window a bit so he could hear the surf from the beach and settled down on the sofa. The sky was a violent mix of orange and scarlet with ribbons of lavender. It was going to be a nice day tomorrow.

He sat enjoying the long stretch of June evening. Sometimes it was good to be alone and not talk or have to think of anything. He refused to think about the future. Because all he had right now was the present moment.

CHAPTER FIVE

*C*aroline was in the dining room of the B & B by eight the following morning. All the other tables were full, but she sat alone at hers. She heard a variety of languages around her. She recognized German and Italian, and the couple at the table next to her was British. It was like the United Nations had sat down for breakfast.

Breda served what she called a full Irish breakfast. There were two eggs over easy, two rashers, one medallion each of black and white pudding, half a broiled tomato, and two slices of toast. Caroline devoured it.

Before she departed, Breda reiterated the directions and Caroline nodded several times, hoping for the best.

She slowly nosed her car out of the driveway and onto the coast road. A quick glance at the beach showed only walkers and some dogs scampering about. There were no windsurfers on the water yet, but the bright blue caravan had just pulled in and was setting up for the day. The sky was overcast, the sea was a gray color, and a mist hovered in the distance, partially obscuring Macgillicuddy's Reeks across the inlet.

The coast road to Dingle town was a more recent road, and

the pavement was even and wide even if it did skirt frighteningly close along the edge of the coastline. Caroline paid close attention to where her car was in relation to the cliff's edge at all times. She didn't think the low guardrail would prevent her from careening over the side of it. The road turned off, heading inland, and the drive turned into a pleasant one through green hills and valleys. The area was not densely populated. There was a variety of houses, from newer bungalow types to older, narrow stone farmhouses. And there were ruins of old cottages and stone outbuildings. She wished someone else was driving so she could enjoy the view and take everything in.

Dingle town was a pleasant surprise. It was a pretty town with its own harbor that backed up against the mountains of the peninsula. A variety of boats were docked in the harbor, and the town itself was a colorful explosion of terraced shops. Caroline found the street where the solicitor was located but noticed there was no parking. Driving further on, she soon spotted a car-park sign and pulled in, leaving the car there and walking back to her destination.

She walked along the sidewalk in front of terraced row houses painted vibrant shades of red, orange, blue, and green. The sounds of seagulls and the harbor bell sounded in the distance. The solicitor's office was located in a terraced house nestled between an ice-cream shop on its right and on its left, a general store with a rack of postcards on the sidewalk out front. The solicitor's name was embossed in black on a brass plaque to the right of his door. She tried the door but it was locked. Glancing to her right, she saw the ice-cream parlor was darkened.

"Gerry doesn't open until ten," said a voice from the general store.

Caroline followed the sound of the voice and saw an elderly man wearing an apron over his short-sleeved shirt, setting out a second rack of postcards.

"You're here to see Gerry Condon? The solicitor?" he asked. When Caroline nodded, he said, "Like I said, he'll be there at ten." With that, he disappeared back into the shop.

Caroline glanced at her watch, figuring she had half an hour or so before he opened. She couldn't stand outside his office like an idiot, so she walked in the direction of the boats. For the next half hour, she walked around the harbor, taking in all the sights and reading information about harbor cruises. She guessed it was a busy town, especially on a warm, sunny day. There was a bit of brightness trying to peek through the clouds, so maybe there would be sun after all.

She arrived back at the solicitor's office about fifteen minutes past ten. The receptionist told her to head on up the stairs.

Gerry Condon was a tall man with dark, curly hair and square black glasses. He wasn't much older than her.

He asked her how she was finding Ireland and how her flight had been, and then got down to particulars. He leaned forward and opened a folder on his desk blotter. "We've received the title back from Dublin, and the deed to the property has been transferred to your name." He handed her a sheet of paper that showed her property carved out. The plot of ten acres was rectangular in shape. There was something oddly satisfying about seeing her name on a deed all by itself. Even if it was on the other side of the world from where she lived.

"What's next?" she asked, anxious to sell it and move on with her life.

The solicitor launched into the topic of capital acquisitions tax and how it was a pity that she wasn't a direct descendant of Maeve's, because then her amount would be less.

Caroline worried about this but before she could ask any questions, the solicitor was onto the next subject.

"You've got a prime location with a view of Inch Beach. You'll have no problem selling it and getting a good price for it.

And it's all in euros, so you'll make money on converting those euros into dollars if the exchange rate remains in your favor."

She hadn't considered the property too much. And she hadn't expected it to have too many pluses. Her intention all along had been not to view it. But as soon as he mentioned the view of the beach, she knew she had to see it.

Impulsively, she asked, "May I see the property?" Maybe she could just drive by to satisfy the small amount of curiosity she had. She didn't want to find anything to like about it that might deter her from her plan.

"Of course," he said. "We can drive out now. Will I call one of the auctioneers in town and see if they would meet us there?"

She nodded. "That would be great."

It was agreed that she would follow Gerry back to Inch. They'd almost arrived at Inch Beach when the solicitor pulled off a small road that she had not noticed before. Her car climbed the ascent with ease, not that far before the solicitor turned down another, narrower lane and pulled his car over to the side of the road. Caroline parked her car behind his, struck by the expansive view of Inch Strand and the Atlantic Ocean spread out before them. She could hear the surf as she got out of her car.

The solicitor waited for her by a gate parked between two low hedges. Caroline was surprised to find a long bungalow, similar to the B & B where she was staying. She'd been expecting a quaint little Irish cottage.

"You're lucky in that the bulk of the property is in the frontage, which is an advantage when you sell. It's a wide plot rather than long and narrow."

Caroline wasn't paying attention, because she couldn't take her eyes off the view of the beach below. She swallowed hard. This was the reason she hadn't wanted to come out here and view the house. She didn't want to find anything to like about it.

ONCE THE REAL ESTATE AGENT—CALLED an auctioneer in Ireland —had arrived, Caroline took a tour of the house with him and the solicitor. The house had been empty for more than a decade, and signs of disuse and ruin were beginning to be evident. But as the auctioneer pointed out, there were no devastating signs of damp. Caroline hadn't even thought about that. But she supposed with a rainy climate, the damp was unavoidable. It was a project, for sure. A project for someone who loved to renovate. Caroline couldn't be that person, not now, not ever, she reminded herself.

The house had its original high ceilings and cove molding throughout. There was faded floral carpeting in all the rooms. The kitchen housed a large hearth with a woodburning stove. The kitchen units were dated but upon inspection, the cabinet doors proved to be hardwood, and Caroline rubbed her hand along the front of one of them, thinking it could be salvaged.

The biggest surprise was to be found in the front room, which overlooked the beach. An original fireplace with an ornate, hand-carved wood surround stood proudly at one end of the space. Caroline examined it up close, admiring the craftsmanship of the intricate Celtic knots. She forced her thoughts away from the flurry of ideas regarding color palettes and upgrades.

"Are you planning on selling as is?" was the first question the auctioneer asked.

"What would you suggest?" she asked, forcing herself to concentrate on maximizing her profit instead of thinking about those wide windows in the front rooms overlooking the beach and the ocean.

The auctioneer was a big, blustery man settled in his mid- to late fifties. Caroline pictured a wife at home and some college-aged kids. He seemed to have "family man" written all over him. She wondered what was written all over her.

"I think if you just tidy it up a bit it might present better. Nothing expensive, but some paint, a good clean, and have all the doors on the kitchen cabinets either fixed or replaced. It might help." He rubbed his chin, looked down at her, and smiled. "But no matter what, you're still going to fetch a great price. It's location, location, location," he said with a laugh.

Caroline folded her arms and sighed. Between taxes and cosmetic work, she'd have to shell out money first before making any. The last thing she needed was for this to turn into a major money pit.

"Is there someone local I could hire to do all this?" she asked. There were only two weeks before she had to return home. If she could get someone right away, then some of the work could be done before she left.

The auctioneer nodded. "Yeah, I know someone. He's a carpenter by trade but a general handyman as well. He can do some basic plumbing and electrical, too, if need be. And most of all, he's trustworthy and he won't gouge you."

"Well, that's good," she said. "How do I get in touch with him?"

"I'll ring him today," the auctioneer said. "Then you'll want to wait to list the property?"

"Yes. Let's get it fixed up." Again, she reminded herself that she was only doing basic cosmetic work. She was not going to get attached to it. She didn't want to go away and start thinking about all the potential and possibility of the place.

Before they left, she asked about getting the utilities turned on. There was running water because there was a well, but there was no electricity. The solicitor said he'd ring the electric company to get it turned on.

Caroline tried not to look at the view when the three of them exited the house, but it was just about impossible when it surrounded them. For the first time since she'd heard she'd inherited the property, it didn't feel like a nuisance. It was going to allow her to do so much back home. Reclaim her life. She smiled to herself, feeling grateful.

Later that evening, the auctioneer rang her at the B & B to tell her that the carpenter would meet her at the property in the morning. She checked her emails again for the hundredth time. Still nothing from the college about the nurse practitioner program that was starting in the fall. When she'd enquired about the program, she'd been disappointed to hear that the application process had been closed but, undaunted, she'd done something she would never have done in the past: she reached out to Dr. Walsh to see if he could pull some strings to get her into the fall program.

She decided to head back out and investigate the beehive huts she'd seen a sign for on the coast road earlier that morning. The day had remained overcast, but crowds still populated the beach. She had to agree with their outlook: who cared what the weather was as long as you were on the beach?

CHAPTER SIX

*P*atrick rolled his work van into his mother's circular driveway late in the afternoon and parked near the front door. There had been some last-minute, unexpected work over in Kenmare, and it had taken him the day to sort it out. He was tired. When he stepped out of his car, he stretched his legs, thinking that once the girls were in bed he'd have an early night.

His house was situated slightly above hers on the hill, all part of the same parcel, land that had been handed down from father to son from generation to generation.

He opened the front door, and Gemma came running down the tiled hallway yelling, "Daddy's here!" She came at him full force, like the launch of a cannon, and landed in his arms. He hugged her tight and kissed her cheek.

"How's my girl?" he asked. No matter how tired he was, his girls always brought a smile to his face.

Gemma placed her little hands on both of his cheeks and contorted her face. "Daddy! You need to shave!"

"I do indeed," he said, setting her back down on the floor. "Is Gran in the kitchen?"

"She's making fairy buns for us. I helped! She said I was a big girl now," Gemma said proudly.

For all her interfering in his own personal life, his mother had been a godsend for the girls. He knew that she hadn't planned on helping to raise young girls at this stage in her life. But she never complained, and the girls loved their gran.

Gemma skipped into the kitchen and Patrick followed her, smiling. There was something about a child skipping; it indicated to him contentedness. Over her shoulder, Gemma said, "And Edel's here, and she brought us sweets!"

Patrick groaned inwardly. He just wasn't up for Edel.

His mother's kitchen was at the back of her house. Hands on his hips, he surveyed the scene laid out before him. His mother sat with Lucy at the table. As his mother iced the cupcakes, his youngest daughter dusted them with a generous amount of chocolate sprinkles. Across from them was Edel, who broke into a broad smile when she spotted him. He returned the smile with a more reserved one of his own, not wanting to be rude. Maureen used to tease him about Edel in a good-natured way. If she could only see what was going on now, how eagerly Edel wanted to step into her shoes. Sometimes it made his head spin.

"Daddy!" Lucy screamed, startling his mother who then burst out laughing.

The younger girl jumped down from her chair and ran to him. Gemma sat in Lucy's now-vacated chair, leaned into her grandmother, and whispered something into her ear. Her grandmother smiled and handed the girl one of the frosted fairy cakes.

"How's the littlest girl in Inch?" he asked, swooping her up into his arms.

"She's a pure rogue," Ada Kelly said with a grin.

"What did you do today?" he asked Lucy hesitantly. Gemma had been an easy child, whereas Lucy enjoyed testing boundaries. The week before, while he'd been outside mowing the grass, she'd taken it upon herself to bake a cake. By the time he came in, there was flour and broken eggs everywhere. The week before that, she'd found an old bottle of Maureen's nail varnish and had tried to paint her nails, along with everything else in the bathroom.

"Hello, Patrick," Edel said from her seat. A few years younger than him, Edel was fairly attractive with her reddish hair and blue eyes. She was very nice, but the problem was she was too quiet for his taste. He could never quite get past the way she'd always seemed to be lurking in the background as they were growing up. He'd been best mates with her older brother for years until her brother went off to Australia, and it had been impossible not to notice Edel crushing on him. Even when he'd married Maureen, she was still there.

He nodded acknowledgement to her. "Edel."

"Lucy locked me in the bathroom," Gemma reported.

"Again?" Patrick asked, exasperated.

Ada looked pointedly at her oldest granddaughter. "I thought that was going to be our secret." Gemma shrugged and with her finger, scraped icing off the top of her bun.

"Lucy," Patrick said.

"And then she ran off with the key and hid it." Ada laughed, shaking her head.

"How did you get her out?"

Ada smiled at Gemma. "Well, with a little bit of coaxing, Gemma managed to climb out of the bathroom window."

"Is the bathroom door still locked?" he asked.

She shook her head. "No. I rang Edel. She came up with a screwdriver and saved the day."

When he looked over at Edel, she smiled and said, "When I was younger, I used to lock my brother in the bathroom, so I guess this is payback for me."

"Lucy, what did you do with the key?" he asked, setting her

down. When she shrugged and said nothing, he held out his hand and said, "Come on, show me where it is."

"It's all right, Patrick," his mother said. "Let her be."

But he took the girl by the hand and led her out of the kitchen. Crouching down to her level, he said softly, "Gran needs the key to her bathroom. And you know it isn't right to take what isn't yours."

He straightened up and as he did, Lucy shot off down the hall toward the back bedrooms. He had an inkling of where she'd hidden the key. And sure enough, she stood at the back door that led out to the garage. There was a doorstop in the figure of a black cat that weighed a ton but was something that the little girl had always been fascinated with. The gold skeleton key glinted in the fading afternoon light, tucked just behind the immovable cat. He smiled at his daughter and picked up the key.

"No more locking your sister in the bathroom," he said. "Or any other room, for that matter."

She broke into a fit of giggles and ran down the hall toward the kitchen.

"Girls, are you ready?" he asked, glancing at the kitchen clock above the range. It was nearing six. He still had to get them their tea, and then baths. His new job was starting at the Burke place in the morning.

"If you wanted to go windsurfing, I'd be more than happy to mind the girls for you," Edel volunteered.

"That's nice of you, Edel," Ada said.

But Patrick knew a conspiracy when he saw one. He shook his head. "I appreciate the offer, Edel, but it's going to be an early night for me." He didn't want to get into the reason why he didn't have a board.

"Oh," was all she said. He did not miss the look of disappointment on his mother's face, and he was relieved when she didn't press the issue. He'd spent the entire day at work installing wood flooring and his knees were now protesting.

"I'm starting work at the Burke place tomorrow," he said casually, rubbing the back of his neck. His mother's and Edel's heads shot up.

"Apparently the American who now owns it wants to fix it up to put it on the market," he explained.

"Pity to sell it," Ada said, shaking her head.

She walked him to the door and helped him carry the girls and all their belongings out to his car. There was Gemma's uniform from the national school where she was in senior infants' class, and then all the toys Lucy liked to take with her. He felt lucky that he didn't have to pay for a crèche or a childminder.

"Did they eat a good dinner?" he asked as he strapped them into their car seats in the back.

Ada stood with her hands on her hips, smiling. "They did. I made bacon and cabbage with mash, and they were hungry. That Lucy loves her carrots."

"Thanks, Ma," he said, hopping into his car.

"Deirdre dropped off a plate to your house earlier. All you have to do is heat it up," she said.

"Thanks again," he said, and as she backed up a few steps, he put his car into drive and eased it down the sloping drive.

The drive to his house was only three minutes, but Lucy still managed to doze off. Gently, he woke her and brought her into the house. He gave them something to eat: Nutella spread on toast and a glass of milk. Then it was bath and bedtime.

Once the girls were in bed, Patrick collapsed on the sofa, too tired to even turn on the television. He gazed out at the vista of Inch Beach spread out before him. The descending grassy slope was covered in a mix of wild, flame-colored montbretia and fuchsia. There were heavy clouds hanging low across the inlet, partially obscuring the purplish haze of Macgillicuddy's Reeks.

But the water itself was flat and silver like a mirror. No one was out on the water.

Maureen came to mind, as she did from time to time. It had gotten better than it had been in the beginning, when she occupied every waking thought. When he did think of her, he was often flooded with guilt. Guilt over the fact that he hadn't been thinking of her, guilt that he had lived and she had died. Guilt that she had been so young. In many ways, he couldn't believe that their marriage was over. Before they'd had a chance to build a substantial history of children and shared memories, she was gone. There were times when he was still overwhelmed with disbelief. They had had so many plans. And then there was the anger. The feeling that his girls had been cheated of their mother. That he had been cheated out of his wife and marriage. He had never felt more helpless in his life than he had since his wife died.

He fell asleep still gazing out at Inch Strand.

PATRICK OVERSLEPT. He rushed through the house, waking the girls and trying to get the breakfast on the table. He made a pot of porridge on the stove, keeping his eye on the clock. Gemma came out first with her uniform on askew. He gave it a quick straightening out, and as she sat down to eat her breakfast, he stood behind her, brushing her hair into a ponytail.

"Come on, Lucy, eat up," he said to his younger daughter, who wasn't fully awake yet.

Standing at the sink, he finished his own bowl of porridge and swallowed down his orange juice in one gulp. From the fridge, he pulled out Gemma's sandwich and apple and threw them into her lunch bag. In ten minutes, he managed to hustle them out of the house, but he had to drop Gemma off at school first so she wouldn't be late, and then take Lucy to his mother's.

Ada was waiting for them at her front door. Patrick lifted Lucy out of her car seat and handed her to his mother.

She ruffled the little girl's hair. "I think someone is not awake. Go away, Patrick, you don't want to be late."

Five minutes later, Patrick arrived at the old Burke place. He muttered under his breath. He was late. He removed his tools from the back of his work van. He whistled as he headed for the front door, which was wide open. He was anxious to get to work.

CHAPTER SEVEN

Caroline glanced at her watch with a sigh, realizing the carpenter was fifteen minutes late. She'd give him another fifteen, and then she'd call the auctioneer and tell him he was a no-show. It was disappointing as she was anxious to get started, and it certainly wasn't a good first impression. She wore clothes she didn't mind getting dirty. Breda at the B & B had already said she could use the wash machine. She stood up and headed to the kitchen at the back of the house to get a better look. The room, unused, was covered in dust. The long window that ran the length of the sink and counter looked out on the sandy-brown scrub of the mountain. A handful of houses were scattered above hers. Up close, she noticed a small back garden overgrown with fuchsia and bluebells. It was not unpretty, it just needed to be cleaned up. At the end of the garden was an old stone outbuilding that was all boarded up. At some point, she'd have to get in there.

With her hands on her hips and biting her lip, she surveyed the rest of the room. It needed a good scrubbing. Even the windows were covered in dust. There was a table and one chair, and she couldn't help but wonder what had happened to the second, third, and fourth. Or had there always been just one? She started opening cabinets and her heart sank. There were crumbs every-where, and rodent droppings. She ran her hands over the cabinet door surfaces, deciding she'd sand them down and stain them. It was a job she was familiar with. But first, basic cleaning needed to be done. She'd have to get to a store and buy a bucket, a mop, and cleaning supplies.

"Hello! Hello!" called someone from the front of the house, startling Caroline.

She rushed forward from the kitchen, thinking it must be the carpenter. She pulled up short when she saw who stood in the doorway.

The man from the beach. The one she had almost run over. *Almost.*

His eyes widened when he recognized her. "It's you," he said.

Ignoring his accusing tone, she extended her hand. "I'm Caroline Egan."

He regarded her warily for a moment before shaking her hand. "Patrick Kelly."

"You're the carpenter?" she asked.

"Well I'm not the door-to-door salesman," he retorted.

She didn't say anything, deciding not to humor him with a reply. There again were those eyes the color of a stormy ocean, and silver threaded through his short brown hair. His arms were tanned and freckled. No doubt about it, he was handsome. Add that delicious Irish accent, and he could be downright dangerous. Could be. *Too bad about his crappy personality*, she thought.

"Mick Corbett rang me last night and said you were looking to fix the place up so you can sell it," he started. He folded his arms across his chest.

"That's the plan. Are you interested?" she asked.

"I'm here, aren't I?" he said.

Caroline blinked, feeling flustered. He was the last person she'd expected to cross her path. She'd assumed she'd never see him again after the other day. Apparently his surly attitude was not just about almost getting hit by a car; it extended to general conversation as well.

"So what is it you need done exactly?" he asked. His tone was brusque.

She dismissed his rudeness. What did it matter? She was going home in less than two weeks.

"I'd like just basic work done," she said. "All the walls and ceilings repainted."

He nodded. "That would include prep work. You know, fill the holes with compound, skim the plaster—"

She cut him off with a slight lift of her chin. "I know. I did a lot of reno work with the house I live in now."

Patrick raised his eyebrows and said nothing.

As they walked room by room through the bungalow, Patrick tucked his pencil behind his ear, removed a tape measure from his tool belt, and took some measurements, scribbling down notes in a small spiral-bound notebook. As he did, Caroline noticed the muscles rippling along his back, underneath his formfitting T-shirt.

In the last bedroom, he nodded toward the faded brown floral carpet. "What about all the carpets and the flooring?"

She sighed. "I suppose it'll need to be ripped up."

"Doesn't make sense to stop at just the walls. The fact that the carpets and floors are in such rough shape would detract from the newly painted walls."

She had to agree with him.

"That'd involve skimming the floor with about a sixteenth of an—"

Caroline nodded quickly.

Patrick gave her a tight smile. "Right. You know. You've done reno work before."

When they did the full circuit, they found themselves back in the front room, standing in front of the large window, gazing out at the beach.

"It's a great location. It's a pity you have to sell it," he said.

It was almost normal conversation.

"It is, but it's no good to me. I don't live here," she explained.

"No, you don't," he agreed.

Caroline stiffened. "Look, again, I apologize for the other day. But unless surly is your default personality, you don't seem to want to be here. Maybe I'd be better off with someone else."

He regarded her for a moment, his expression blank. "Are you hiring me to get the reno work done or are you looking for scintillating conversation?"

Caroline rolled her eyes and changed the subject. "I'm hoping to have it ready to list by the time I head back to the States," she said.

"When's that?" he asked, turning to her. His gray eyes were stippled with gold. The sunlight streaming in through the window shone off the silver highlights of his dark hair.

"Two weeks," she replied, forcing her gaze away from his face. She did not want to find him attractive.

He snorted. "Not a hope. You expect me to have all this work done in that time frame?"

She bristled. "I'm not sure how fast you work, so you tell me."

"Well, I don't work that fast," he said. "My best estimate would be about two months."

"Two months?" she said. "I can't stay here that long." And she couldn't. Kevin was pressing to buy out her half of the house. This could really stretch her finances. Once the severance payout was depleted, she'd have to dip into her savings and then her retirement account, and she really didn't want to do that. And though she hadn't yet heard whether she'd been accepted to the college program, she was still hoping she'd have the fall semester of school to prepare for.

"You don't need to be here," he said.

Caroline ignored his comment. She bit her lip. "What if I do some of the work myself, then? Would that help move things along?"

Hands on his hips, Patrick regarded her evenly with a raised eyebrow. "Can you work a drill? A hammer? Hang a door?"

Caroline sighed in exasperation, getting the sense that he was either trying to tease her or frustrate her or quite possibly both. "Probably not hang doors, but I have used a drill before, and you could show me—"

He was shaking his head before she even had the whole sentence out of her mouth. "By the time I show you what to do, I could have done it myself."

She had no reply for him, because she could see his point. "All right, two months then. You'd be here every day?"

"Yes."

"Weekends?"

Patrick shook his head. "No, I have previous commitments."

She wondered if that included a wife or girlfriend. There was no wedding ring on his finger. But that didn't necessarily mean anything.

They haggled over a price and eventually came to an agreement and shook on it. Caroline said she'd get something written up for him to sign.

He shrugged. "If that makes you feel better. I was just going to write up an estimate for you."

"I don't care," Caroline said, frustrated. "When can you start?"

"I can start right now," he said.

"Okay, great." She turned to walk away, but he called out her name. She turned and met his steely gaze.

"I have two conditions of my own," he said.

"Yes?"

"You can either pay me fifty percent down or pay me weekly until the end of the job," he said.

She nodded. "Whichever you prefer."

"Weekly, then," he said.

"And the other condition?"

"I only ask that you try not to kill, maim, or injure me," he said, and then without another word, he brushed past her, whistling, heading out to his car.

She stared after him, her mouth hanging open.

CAROLINE DIDN'T HEAD BACK to the B & B immediately after she left the house. She drove back down to Dingle and did some shopping, mainly for cleaning supplies. Until the electricity was turned on, there wasn't much she could do at the house. The shopping didn't take long, and she found herself staring at her watch. She was in no hurry to get back to her accommodation, because it was still light out, and she wasn't ready to sit in her room all night. She stopped at a restaurant and ordered some dinner, trying to ignore the feelings of self-consciousness that pervaded her as she sat alone. Nervously, she looked around at the other diners. She told herself she'd better get used to it, because that was the status of her life for the foreseeable future: single.

Before sunset, Caroline headed back to the B & B, anxious not to be driving alone on the coastal road in the dark. Once inside her room, she realized she was annoyed with herself and the Irishman. She'd never met anyone so rude. Not that she would have expected to become best friends with the tradesman, but was it too much to ask for someone to be polite and courteous? The more she thought about it, the more she realized she didn't have to put up with that kind of behavior. She picked up her phone off the desk and scrolled through her contacts, then rang the auctioneer.

This was a delicate subject, so she had to proceed carefully. "Um, yes, I was wondering if you had another carpenter you could recommend?"

He hesitated and then asked, "Is there a problem with Patrick? Is he unable to do the work?"

"No, it isn't that," she stammered. How did she tell him that she found the man irritating, that he was rude to her, that she had almost run him over? All she wanted was to get the house into shape to sell it; she needed no unnecessary aggravation.

"Then what?" the auctioneer pressed. "You'd be hard-pressed to find a better carpenter than Patrick. Our community here at Inch is small, and we all look out for each other."

"I can certainly understand your loyalty to a member of your community, but as I'm not a member of this community, it doesn't apply to me," she explained. She wanted to pat herself on the back for such a professional, straightforward response. She wasn't usually able to think that fast on her feet.

"How about compassion? Do you possess any of that?" he asked.

"Excuse me?" she asked, wondering what that had to do with any of this.

The auctioneer sighed on the other end of the line. "We all look out for Patrick because of his situation."

"Situation?"

"Didn't he mention it?" the auctioneer asked.

"No," she replied, curious.

He hesitated. "It's common knowledge, so I guess it won't be a problem for me to share it."

As she waited, she realized she was holding her breath.

"He lost his wife a few years ago," the auctioneer explained.

"He's been trying to get his bearings ever since. That's why I throw him everything that comes my way, workwise."

"Oh," she said.

"Look, think about it, and if you still want another carpenter, ring me back," he instructed, then said goodbye and hung up.

Caroline was left staring at her phone for a good minute. *Oh.*

It explained some things. If there was one thing Caroline had, it was compassion. After all, Patrick was still young. And to lose your spouse so early . . . She shook her head. What a shame. She was stuck with the carpenter, but at least she had a reason for his moodiness. It didn't excuse his behavior, but it did explain it.

After she showered and put on her pajamas, she checked the time. It was half ten and it was only just getting dark outside.

As she lay on the bed, she turned on her laptop and saw an email from the college where she'd applied for her nurse practitioner degree. She clicked open the email and scanned it, then let out a whoop and a holler when she read that she'd been accepted into their program for the fall. Dr. Walsh had said he would do whatever he could, and he had kept his word. It was the best news she'd heard in a long time. All thoughts of the Irishman fell away from her mind.

THERE WAS nothing that could put Caroline in a bad mood the following morning, not even the surly carpenter. She was still riding the high of being accepted into the nurse practitioner program back home. The sooner she got this house fixed up and sold, the better. The electricity had been turned on at the house, and that put her in an even better mood.

She was in the kitchen, deciding where to start, when Patrick arrived. He came through the open front door, whistling and carrying a large toolbox.

"I'm going to start prepping the walls for painting," he said. No "hello," "how are you," or anything civil like that.

Caroline nodded. Her plan was to give the place a good clean before she started the actual work. She filled the bucket in the sink. She was going to wash the cabinet doors and wipe out the shelves in the cupboards before she started any sanding.

Patrick stood in the doorway, filling it. "You might want to wait until after we're finished before you start washing down walls and windows and such," he remarked.

"I prefer to give it a quick clean before I start working," she explained.

"Suit yourself," he said.

"I will," she said sweetly.

He walked away toward the back bedrooms, shaking his head.

The farther away the better, she thought. From afar she could hear him whistling. Funny, he didn't strike her as a whistler.

When the bucket water had turned a gray color, she walked out the front door and dumped it down the drain. A small white postal van with "An Post" emblazoned in green and gold on the side of it drove up and parked out front.

The postman stepped out of the vehicle and walked through the gate in the front hedge. He strolled up the path toward her, hands in his pockets. Caroline set the bucket down and wiped her hands on her shorts.

"You must be the Yank who Maeve Burke left her property to," was the conversation opener. His face was square, his eyes wide-set, and his features flat. He had a crop of curly, graying hair that reminded Caroline of Julius Caesar.

"I am," she said, offering her hand. "Caroline Egan."

He shook her hand with his own beefy one. "Frank Dolan, your postman."

"I won't be here long enough to get mail," she told him.

He grinned. "You never know."

It occurred to Caroline that she didn't know the address of her property. She couldn't recall seeing a street sign.

"You know, Frank, I don't even know what my address is," she admitted. "What's the name of this street we're on?"

He scratched the back of his head. "The road has no name. You live in the townland of Ballymann. Your address is Ballymann, Inch, County Kerry. That will do." He added with a laugh, "And your name of course."

He was so genial she couldn't help but smile.

"It will?" she asked. Somehow that address seemed sparse. Lacking.

He nodded. "Whatever you do, don't put Inch Beach," he advised. "The last postman used to deliver any piece of post or parcel that had 'Inch beach' written on it, directly onto the beach below." The postman did not hide his disgust. He gave a sniff and said, "But then Dev could always be awkward like that."

Although she tucked away what he'd told her, she knew it wasn't necessary. She'd be going home soon.

The postman continued. "Or you could name the place. But whatever you do, don't name it anything like Seaview Cottage or Oceanview House. I've got four or five of each on my route, and it's pure bedlam at Christmastime with all the cards."

"I won't be here long enough to name it," she said.

"In that case, you've got no decisions to make." He smiled, bid her goodbye, and walked to his postal van.

THE FOLLOWING MORNING, Patrick was already at the Burke place when Caroline arrived. He sat on the back bumper of his white work van, drinking from a thermos.

Their eyes met, but neither spoke at first.

"You're already here," she said. She popped the trunk of the rental car and began to remove more cleaning supplies she'd picked up in Tralee: a mop, a broom, and other supplies. Breda's husband, Joe, had been going to Tralee himself, on the other side of the peninsula, and had offered to take her there.

"I'd like to get started," Patrick said, capping his thermos bottle and setting it in the back of his van. He walked over to her. "Can I carry those in for you?"

"No thanks, I can manage." She slammed the trunk closed.

As she unlocked the front door, Patrick said, "Maybe you could give me a key to get in."

When she didn't say anything, he muttered, "It's not like I'm going to steal anything. Not that there's anything to steal."

She pulled up short in her tracks. Would they begin every day with an argument? It was already beginning to wear on her. "It's not that I don't trust you, Patrick," she said. "I don't even know you."

"If you need a reference, I can get you several," he pressed.

"Not necessary," she said, and that was all she said. She unlocked the front door and it swung open. She carried her things inside and through to the kitchen in the back. Over her shoulder, she said, "Besides, I only have one key."

Patrick set his toolbox down in the front room.

"I'll take the measurements for the doors; they'll need to be ordered," he said, thinking aloud.

She nodded. "How does that work? Do I pay you, or do I need to go with you to order them?"

"I have an account, so I'll order them and you can reimburse me," he said. "You're also going to need a skip. I'll order that as well. A small one will do."

Caroline set the bucket down on the floor and leaned the mop, still in plastic wrap, against the wall. She stood with her hands on her hips.

"What room will you be working in?" Caroline asked. She felt like she was ready to take on the world, but she wanted to take it on with him as far away as possible.

Patrick scratched the back of his neck and looked around. "I was going to start removing the doors. I can start in the bedrooms."

"That's great," she said brusquely. "I'll be here. I'll keep out of your way."

He nodded. His phone rang and he retrieved it from his pocket. "Yeah?" He headed back to the bedrooms while talking on the phone. "Yeah, yeah. No, don't let her do that. I'm trying to break her of that."

It was hard not to listen, and Caroline found herself wondering who the "her" was. A dog, maybe? It sounded like it, but he didn't strike her as a dog type. She was a cat person herself, and she had always wanted to get one, but Kevin had had severe allergies. She smiled to herself as she set the bucket in the sink, squirted some detergent into it, and turned on the faucet. Once she returned home, she was going to get a cat, she decided. A cat would be far better suited to her lifestyle than a dog. Dogs were too needy. Cats were more independent.

When thoughts of the carpenter drifted before her, she forced herself to think about her future. School, the house, a cat or maybe even two. Because she was so done with men.

CHAPTER EIGHT

*P*atrick was unsettled. Of all people, he had not expected the American woman at the Burke place. His impression of her had changed only slightly from their first encounter on the beach. It seemed she was going to sell the place as soon as she could to make a quick profit.

By the weekend, Deirdre had been keen for news about the new owner of the Burke place, and he had mumbled a few dismissive words about it being someone who just wanted to sell it. Mercifully, she dropped the topic of conversation once she realized he was in poor humor, recognizing the signs of him needing to be alone. Agitated, he'd paced back and forth in his living room, oblivious to night falling outside.

The problem was that despite having an initial poor impression of her, he found her attractive. And that made him nervous. Since Maureen's death, he had been attracted to a few women. He wasn't a monk after all. But he hadn't had to work with any of them. He was going to be spending every day together with this woman for the next two weeks. When she'd said she'd only be there for a short time, a fleeting thought had run through his mind: what would be the harm? A little fling. But as soon as he'd returned to his car to get his toolbox, he'd caught sight of the girls' car seats and guilt had seared through him.

Since Maureen died, Patrick had gone on a total of two dates. And both had been disastrous. He'd kept comparing the women to his late wife, thinking, *Maureen wouldn't have said that* or *Maureen wouldn't have done that.* The dates had been set up by well-meaning friends and loved ones who thought he should move on with his life. They couldn't understand at the time how he couldn't go forward and leave his wife behind. He hadn't been ready. He might never be ready.

"Daddy, can I have a drink of water?" Lucy asked, standing in the doorway.

"What?" He turned around, relieved at the distraction. He was pulled back to reality and in two strides was at her side, lifting her up in his arms. Patrick carried Lucy to the kitchen, filled a cup with a bit of water, and gave it to her. She drank it promptly.

After Patrick tucked Lucy back into her bed, his thoughts wandered toward his children. No one could replace Maureen as their mother. No one. That was another reason he wasn't so eager about dating. It wasn't just about himself anymore. He couldn't make any major life decisions without taking his girls into account. He was very conscious of that.

He stood in the doorway of the girls' bedroom watching Lucy trying to get comfortable, but it wasn't long before she was fast asleep. Gemma was a great sleeper, always had been since she was a baby. But she also always managed to kick off her blankets. Glancing over at her, he saw that tonight was no different. He smiled a small smile to himself. Her bare legs hung almost over the edge of the bed. That used to bother Maureen. She was always afraid they'd be cold. Once the girls were sorted, he headed back out to the living room. He was tired, but his mind wouldn't settle down. It would be a long time before he went to sleep.

The best thing to do, he decided, was to play it cool with the

American. Ignore her as much as possible. Just get the job done and collect a paycheck, he told himself. That's all. He was grateful she lived three thousand miles away and was going home within weeks. It was a good thing. Her blonde hair, her big blue eyes, and her hourglass figure would definitely be his undoing if she were to stay any longer.

THE SKIP HAD ARRIVED Monday morning. Patrick instructed them to put it at the end of the driveway next to the house, so the remainder of the driveway was clear for his work van. He spent the rest of the morning removing picture hooks and nails from the walls of the bungalow. After that was done, he went around filling the holes and gaps with compound. By noon, he'd run out of compound and was hungry for lunch. He thought he might head over to his mother's for a meal and to see Lucy.

Caroline stood out front, hands on hips, taking in the view of the beach below. The late morning light cast her in silhouette, and Patrick could see that she was all curves. Serious curves. Dangerous curves. An estimated set of her measurements floated before his eyes. He blinked hard. To distract himself, he began to go through his mental checklist of what he needed to pick up from the general hardware store.

Caroline turned around when she heard him approach.

"I've got to go out and get some more compound, and then I'm going to lunch," he said. "I'll be back in an hour."

"Are you totally out of compound?" she asked.

He nodded.

"Couldn't you just use toothpaste?"

"Toothpaste?" he repeated, scowling.

She nodded. "I've used it in a pinch."

He snorted. "If it's all the same to you, I'll go pick up some compound. Thanks for the Pinterest life hack, though."

He thought he heard her growl behind him, and that put a smile on his face.

~

PATRICK FOUND Lucy and his mother out back, tending to the vast vegetable garden.

"That's a good girl now," Ada said as she directed the four-year-old in the watering of the garden. Lucy had a small pink watering can and ran up and down the rows, water sloshing everywhere. It wasn't only the vegetables that were getting watered.

"Daddy!" she squealed, dropping the watering can and launching into him. He lifted her up and swung her in the air, and she laughed. "How's my girl?"

"Oh, there you are," Ada said. "I was wondering if we'd see you for lunch."

They all traipsed inside to the kitchen. Ada, originally from County Carlow, was the daughter of farmers, and the main dinner was always consumed midday. Patrick used the bathroom and gave his hands a good scrub to get the splatters of compound off of them.

Lucy was climbing into her booster seat when Patrick arrived at the table. Something smelled good. He pushed Lucy's chair in closer to the table and looked over to the stove, squinting to see what was for dinner.

"It's just a roast chicken today," his mother said.

He laughed at the word "just." Ada set a plate before him of sliced chicken breast, a mixed mash of carrot, parsnip, and turnip, and a few broccoli florets. She set down a small plate in front of her granddaughter.

"Be a good girl and eat your dinner, and then I'll give you a sweet," she said, ruffling Lucy's blonde hair.

She returned with a plate of boiled potatoes. Patrick peeled the potatoes using his fork and knife. He set half a steaming potato on his daughter's plate and mashed it up with a pat of butter. Then he peeled two more for his mother and laid them on her plate as she sat down. In quick succession, he peeled three potatoes for himself, mashing butter, salt, and pepper into them with his fork.

With his eyes on the clock, he dug in. He didn't want to stay too late; the American woman was paying him good money.

"What's she like?" Ada asked.

"Who?" he asked, but he knew whom she referred to.

"The American woman," she said.

He shrugged, forking up a bit of chicken, potato, and gravy into his mouth. "She's all right. It's a job."

"She's going to sell it, isn't she?" his mother said with her mouth set in a grim line. Ada Kelly was old school. You didn't sell land. You hung onto it. Forever. It was part of the Irish psyche. The Irish had gone too many centuries unable to own their own land. Now, they owned it and they didn't get rid of it. No matter what. It got passed down from generation to generation. The land was everything.

"It's nothing to her, Ma, she's a blow-in," he said, using the term for an outsider. "What good is it to her to have a property on the other side of the world?"

Mrs. Kelly still wasn't convinced. "She could use it as a holiday home."

He shook his head, shoveling more food into his mouth. "That wouldn't be economically sound. I mean, she can't hardly come down every weekend." He didn't understand why he felt the need to defend her. In the back of his mind, a red flag went up.

Patrick went quiet and finished his dinner. He needed to get back to the Burke place.

After he thanked his mother for dinner and kissed Lucy good-bye, he pulled out and headed back to work. When he pulled up in front of the Burke place, he was surprised to see a newer-model dark sedan parked out in front of the hedge. Caroline stood nearby with her arms crossed over her chest, talking to a man in a suit. She laughed at something the man said, looking pretty and confident, her long blonde hair shining like honey in the mid-afternoon sun. It troubled Patrick that he noticed.

Abruptly, he jumped out of the car, causing Caroline and the suit to glance his way. As he trotted up to the house, he saw that the man held a folder in his hands. From a distance, Patrick could see that there was some kind of logo brandished across the front, but he was still too far away to read it.

He nodded a quick hello and walked past them into the house. Curious, he started working in the front room, where he could hear what they were saying. He wondered who this guy was. He guessed it had to do with selling the property.

"If I am selling the property, what interest does OHG have?" he heard Caroline ask.

Not OHG, Patrick thought with a groan. Anyone but them. OHG stood for Overseas Holiday Group, a company based outside of Ireland who specialized in holiday homes and housing estates here and in the UK and Europe. With a trowel, he slapped compound over the holes in the sitting-room walls. He knew of OHG's reputation: they were developers who'd started several projects throughout the country but hadn't finished them, leaving ghost estates behind. A couple of mates who'd worked for them were still owed money. They were bad business all around.

"I love the Yanks. They just get right to the point," said the man in the suit.

Patrick rolled his eyes.

"And is there a point to your visit?" Caroline said.

Patrick smiled to himself at her cheekiness.

The suit laughed and said, "There is, actually. OHG might be interested in purchasing your property, Miss Egan," he said.

"Call me Caroline," she said. "Purchasing my property for what purpose?"

"OHG is a developer of properties abroad and at home," he said. "This site is unique in that there's more frontage than width. OHG might be interested in purchasing your property for the purpose of building some holiday homes. Maybe eight or ten. Of course, everything would be dependent on planning permission." He paused and added, "No planning permission, no purchase offer."

Patrick grumbled. That's just what they needed. Holiday homes. It would spoil an unspoiled view.

"I understand," she said. "You've certainly given me something to think about."

Don't do it, Caroline, Patrick thought. *Don't sell your soul to a developer. Sell it if you must, but sell it to someone who will love it and appreciate it. Not someone looking to make a quick profit.*

"Look, here's my card," the man in the suit said. "Give me a ring and let me know when the property goes on the market."

"I will," she said. "Would planning permission be hard to get?"

The man gave a small laugh. "Let's just say it can be difficult, but it can also be a case of who you know."

Typical, thought Patrick. They were just going to grease some palms.

"Got it," she said. "Thanks for stopping."

Patrick heard the car starting and then pulling away with a toot of the horn.

From the window, he watched as Caroline lingered, her hand

shielding her eyes from the blazing afternoon sun as she looked down at the beach. He wondered if she could ever feel about this place as he did. There was nowhere else he'd rather be or live.

After a bit, she drifted in with the folder in her hands. She was smiling.

"Who was that?" he asked, compound in one hand, trowel in the other.

"A developer from OHG," she replied. She stepped closer to him. He swallowed hard. Big blue eyes looked up at him, and he felt himself starting to get lost.

Pulling himself together, he cleared his throat and said, "That's just what we need: another developer."

The openness in her face closed down and was replaced with a scowl. "I have to do what's best for me," she said tightly.

"That's right," he said with a bitter laugh. "Every man for himself."

Caroline didn't speak to him for the rest of the day, and he was surprised to find that it bothered him.

CHAPTER NINE

Caroline tried to keep contact with Patrick to a minimum, but it was just about impossible when they were working in such close quarters. More than anything, she wanted to avoid the hassle he insisted on giving her. She could understand that he had been through a rough time, but it almost felt like he was taking his grief out on her personally. If she'd known him better, she would have suggested a grief counselor. Gently, of course.

She'd finished scrubbing the kitchen. Every day she was there, she flung the windows and the doors wide open, and the musty air of the disused bungalow began to dissipate. The sea breeze commingled with the detergent's lemon scent and the house began to feel fresh. It was starting to reclaim its life. She could almost hear the house breathing a sigh of relief. She took a step back from her thought process. No getting attached to the place, she reminded herself. That was the problem when you were hands on with a renovation project; it was hard not to get involved and take it personally. She could not even begin to move in that direction. She picked up a screwdriver and began removing the knobs from the cabinets.

On his way out, Patrick grunted a goodbye and said he'd see her in the morning. She didn't even stop what she was doing or bother to turn around. She didn't have the energy to be kind to him.

Later that evening, after she'd returned to the B & B and cleaned up, Caroline decided to grab something to eat and then head to the beach. Her shoulders ached and she didn't want to venture far from her room at the B & B. She drove up to the nearest petrol station and bought a ready-made sandwich, a packet of cookies, and a banana. She wasn't that hungry, and it would hold her until breakfast.

Down at the beach, the wind had picked up considerably, and the sun had disappeared behind heavy cloud cover. The beach was thinly populated, and Caroline was glad she'd brought her light-weight coat. On a solitary stroll, she headed down the beach. She thought about her plans to go back to school, which excited her, and about being able to buy Kevin out of his half of the house, which relieved her. There was going to be life after Kevin, and it was going to be good.

Caroline loved how the evenings here were light until late at night. When she'd climbed into bed the previous night near eleven, there was still a pearly gray light filtering through the curtains in her room.

From afar, she could see a man flying a kite with two young girls beside him, jumping and clapping as they looked up to the sky where their red, orange, and yellow kite was getting whipped around by the wind. The colorful tail fluttered in the breeze.

The man gave the handle to the older of the two girls but as soon as he let go, the wind proved to be too strong for the girl and lifted the spool out of her hands. Her father grabbed it before it flew off for good. Once he had it back in hand, he stood behind her and kept a firm grip on it.

Caroline sat on the sand and finished her sandwich. She

pulled open the packet of cookies and began munching on one. As the trio neared her, she paused, recognizing Patrick Kelly. He had children! This surprised her. When she'd learned he was a widower, she had never even considered whether he had children. As unobtrusively as possible, she observed him interacting with his daughters. The younger child couldn't be more than three or four. They were so young. Caroline was moved to immediate pity for them.

This was a Patrick she did not know. As the three of them ran with the kite high in the air, he laughed and encouraged his daughters to keep up. There was an ease and a familiarity between the three of them, as well as something else. Joy. That's what it was. Caroline was relieved to see that his person-ality wasn't always surly. Maybe he was only testy with her. For whatever reason, she seemed to bring out the worst in him. At the house, he was brusque, guarded, and snarky. *It must be me*, she thought sourly. He looked freer than she had ever seen him. And she knew that moments like these would help him heal.

As they got closer, Caroline looked away so as not to intrude on their privacy. She ate another cookie and out of the corner of her eye, she noticed the younger girl running toward her. She wished she wouldn't. She held her breath, hoping the young girl would return to Patrick.

"Lucy!" Patrick called out after her, but the young girl laughed and landed at Caroline's feet.

Caroline peeled her banana and was about to take a bite, but the young girl's blue eyes were on her. The older girl approached her, but several times she stopped and looked back at her father as if to seek reassurance. When Caroline's eyes met Patrick's gaze, she saw that he had recognized her. His smile disappeared.

The little girl plopped down beside her. Her tiny feet, shod in white sandals, kicked up some sand.

Caroline didn't know what to say to her, so she held out the packet of cookies. "Would you like a cookie?"

The little girl named Lucy shook her head, smiling, and said, "I'd rather have your banana."

Caroline laughed. She handed it over to the young girl.

The girl took a bite, looked at Caroline, and announced, "It's yellowlicious."

Caroline grinned, amused. By this time, the older daughter had arrived at Caroline's feet. Patrick reeled the kite in and joined them.

"Lucy!" he said. "I'm sorry, did she take your banana?"

Caroline looked up at him, taking in those eyes the color of granite, that square jaw. "No, I offered it to her."

"She's going through a banana phase," he explained.

She nodded. "I understand."

The older girl regarded her with curiosity, playing absent-mindedly with her ponytail. She gave Caroline a shy smile, revealing some missing front teeth. She was the image of her father with her brown hair and those same gray eyes. She eyed the packet of cookies. Caroline picked them up and offered them to her. The girl automatically shook her head, but it didn't convince Caroline. "They're delicious. Are you sure you won't try one?"

The girl put her finger in her mouth and looked back at her father, who nodded.

As children went, they were adorable.

She finally looked back to Patrick, who looked so relaxed in the presence of his daughters. The lines that etched his face didn't seem so deep, and the cloud that usually hung over him seemed to have lifted. Overall, he appeared softer.

"How are you, Caroline?" he asked. His relaxed expression disappeared, and his usual mask of cool detachment settled back into place.

"I'm well."

"These are my girls," he said proudly. "This here is Gemma, and the little lady eating your banana is Lucy."

"They're lovely," she said truthfully.

"Thank you," he said.

"And my name is Caroline," she said to the girls.

"Your voice sounds funny," Gemma said, finishing her cookie.

"Gemma!" Patrick said. "That's not very polite."

The girl's eyes welled up, and Caroline spoke quickly. "I bet my voice does sound funny. It's called an accent. I'm from America, and this is how we sound."

The tears that had threatened to fall disappeared, and the young girl regarded her with awe.

"Do you know where America is?" Caroline asked.

Gemma pointed toward the water. "Far away, on the other side of the ocean."

"That's right. It's far away. And your voice sounds different to me," Caroline said. When the girl giggled, she smiled.

"I never met an American before," Gemma admitted with wonder.

Caroline smiled. "Well, now you have."

There was an awkward silence that threatened to expand around them, and Caroline brushed off her hands and hugged her knees.

"Come on, girls, let's go," Patrick said. "Say goodbye to Caroline."

"Will you fly the kite with us?" Lucy asked, excited.

Even Gemma bit her lip and smiled.

Caroline hesitated. "Oh, I don't know." She didn't want to intrude on their family time.

Lucy jumped up and down and clapped her hands. "Please. Please say yes."

Uncertain, Caroline glanced over at Patrick, who shrugged and said, "Sure, why not?"

"All right, then," she said, hopping up and brushing sand off the seat of her pants and the back of her thighs. "I haven't flown a kite since I was a kid." She looked at Gemma, made a funny face and said, "And that was a long, long time ago." Gemma giggled in response.

Caroline gathered her belongings and joined Patrick and his daughters.

"Did you like flying the kite?" Caroline asked Gemma.

The older girl nodded enthusiastically. "I do. But it's hard. I need big hands like Daddy."

Caroline agreed with her. "When the wind is strong, I bet it would even be hard for me."

"Well, let's find out," Patrick said. He took Lucy gently by her hand. He knelt down until he was eye level with her and said, "Will we watch Caroline fly the kite?"

Lucy nodded.

"Gemma, would you mind holding my purse for me?" Caroline asked.

The older girl took Caroline's purse and looped it over her shoulder.

Patrick handed Caroline the kite spool and their eyes locked. Caroline's lips parted slightly, and he bit his lip before looking away.

"Go on, Caroline," he urged. "I'll get the kite up and we'll start heading back."

Caroline started at a slow trot until the kite was airborne. The wind was so fierce she had to keep both her hands on the spool. Gusts threatened, again and again, to lift it out of her hands. It wasn't long before her upper arms began to ache. She slowed down to a walk, and the kite flew higher and higher.

Patrick and the girls walked amiably along with her. They

chatted about everything and nothing. Caroline was busy trying to prevent the kite from flying away from her—an exercise she found both exhausting and exhilarating—although it was pleasant eavesdropping on their little family circle.

A strong gust lifted the kite higher and Caroline tightened her grip on the spool, but the wind was stronger.

"Oh no!" she said as she struggled. Her arms rose in a desperate attempt to hang on as the spool was pulled away.

"Don't let go of our kite," Gemma said, panic in her voice.

That's just what she didn't want to do was to lose their kite.

Immediately, Patrick was behind her, wrapping her in an embrace as he reached up to rescue the kite. Caroline tried not to notice the warmth of his body or the strength of his arms. But it was impossible. She almost whimpered. It had been a long time since a man had made her feel like that.

"I got it, I got it," he said in a reassuring tone.

Once he'd secured the spool, Caroline slipped out from under his embrace. She wiped her hands on her shorts.

He pulled the kite in and announced, "I think that's enough kite flying for today." He regarded Caroline and said with a laugh, "I think it's time for ice cream."

The girls jumped up and down and clapped their hands. Caroline thought she'd never deserved an ice-cream cone more than she did at that moment.

THEY HEADED BACK toward the car park. Caroline's arms and shoulders ached, but it had been good fun. It was still light out, but the crowd on the beach had thinned.

The four of them walked together up to the café, which also served ice cream, and Patrick set the kite down and bought four ice-cream cones. They carried their cones to an empty picnic bench out front.

The girls didn't seem to mind her presence; they seemed to take it in their stride. Patrick sat across from her. Caroline felt oddly nostalgic for the good parts of her own childhood. Never with her own parents but with her grandmother, who used to treat her to ice cream during the summer. It was such a pleasant recollection in a sea of not-so-pleasant childhood memories.

She glanced over at Gemma, whose scoop of ice cream was beginning to tilt. Melted ice cream ran down the sides of the girl's cone. Out of the corner of her eye, Gemma watched Caroline eat her cone, almost mimicking her.

"Try it like this," she said to Gemma. Caroline tilted her cone slightly and licked around the edge, wiping up any ice cream drips.

Gemma tried it, her face a mask of intense concentration. When she finished, she smiled and announced, "I did it." She had a smear of ice cream on her chin.

"Well done, Gemma." Caroline smiled. She turned her gaze to Patrick, who was staring at her, lost in thought. His features had softened. She swallowed. It was so hard not to be attracted to him. The chiseled features. The day-old beard. The cleft in his chin and the dimple in his cheek. And most of all, those gray eyes. He had a haunted look. A melancholia that she itched to relieve. To comfort.

The girls handed their unfinished cones to their father, who promptly ate them. He looked sheepish when he saw Caroline watching him. "It's one of the fringe benefits of being a father. You get all the leftovers. You're almost never hungry."

"Are you going to be our new mother?" Gemma asked Caroline, eyes bright and intent.

Patrick's mouth opened, but Caroline spoke before he could. "No, I'm just a friend."

The answer seemed to satisfy Gemma, and she took Lucy by the hand and ran off to play in the sand dunes.

Patrick turned on the bench to look out at the ocean.

Caroline couldn't help but wonder what had happened to their mother that had left him alone raising two daughters.

An easy silence settled between them. Caroline was never one of those people that had to be talking to fill the silent spaces.

Patrick looked down at the bench and began to trace the wood grain with his finger. He did not look up when he spoke. "My wife died during childbirth. Everything that could go wrong that day did go wrong," he started, his voice low. "Maureen hadn't felt well that morning. She'd decided to stay home from work. She still had six weeks until her due date. I was over in Killarney on a job site when she called to say she had rung my mother to take her to the hospital. Said she was bleeding. A lot. I left work immediately to meet them at the hospital, but I got a tire puncture just outside Kilorglin." He shook his head. "It's funny how you remember specific things about days that are traumatic. It was pouring rain and I was lying on the side of the road, trying to change the tire, and by the time I arrived at the hospital, I was soaking wet."

He went quiet. Caroline said nothing but did not remove her eyes from him. Sometimes people had to tell their story in their own way. In their own time.

"By the time I got there, they'd already taken her in for an emergency C-section. The placenta had ruptured," he explained. "Lucy weighed in at five pounds even, and she was a fighter." He smiled at the memory of his tiny baby girl, but the smile soon disappeared and a shadow darkened his face. "Maureen wasn't right after the surgery. You know how you just know?" he asked.

Caroline nodded, because she did know. One of the first lessons she'd learned in nursing was to trust your instinct. Most nurses just "knew" when their patient wasn't right. It was almost like a sixth sense.

"After the surgery, she was so pale and weak. They kept saying it was because of everything she'd been through. But she wasn't right and no one would listen." He bent his head, shaking it in frustration.

He drew in a deep breath to recall the rest of it. "The phone rang in the middle of the night." He stopped and looked up to her. "I knew before I even answered it that Maureen was dead." He shook his head again and let out a brittle laugh. "I just knew."

Caroline refrained from reaching out and placing her hand over his. "It must have been absolutely devastating."

"She'd hemorrhaged out. Apparently, they'd nicked an artery during surgery. By the time they found her in the room, she was already gone."

"That is just terrible," she said quietly. And it was.

"It was. Is," he said. He looked away, narrowing his eyes. His profile was a mask of anguish.

Neither said a word. A shadow of melancholy settled in around them. The air seemed chillier, and Caroline pulled her sweater tighter around her.

"That's why I was so angry at you for almost running me down," he explained. He glanced over at his daughters running up and down the grassy sand dunes. "Everything I do, every decision I make, they are my first priority. And I try to be careful about everything. Maureen's death has put everything into laser-sharp focus."

"Of course," she said. Everything was starting to make sense now. She regarded him with sadness.

He glanced at her and grimaced. "Aw, jeez, Caroline," he said, running his hands through his hair.

"What?" she asked, noting his use of her given name. A feeling of lightness fanned throughout her body.

"Please don't pity me," he pleaded.

"I don't feel sorry for *you,* Patrick, but I do feel sorry for the situation you're in, you and your daughters," she said.

"Is there a difference?"

Before she could reply, the girls ran back to the picnic table, breathless, laughing, their hair flying about.

Patrick clapped his hands. "Right then, we should get home. It's getting late."

"Aww," Gemma and Lucy whined in unison.

Patrick stood up from the table, stretching. "Do you need a lift back to your B & B?" he asked.

Caroline shook her head, sorry for the evening to come to an end. "No, I have my car with me."

"All right, I'll see you in the morning," he said with a nod. "Girls, say goodnight to Caroline."

"Bye!" they shouted as they walked off, hand in hand with their father.

Caroline didn't leave right away. She sat quietly at the picnic table, watching the ocean roll in and out, listening to the sounds of the surf and the lone seagull. She was thinking about Patrick and his girls. She had enjoyed the kite flying and the ice-cream cone. She had enjoyed Patrick's company. She had even enjoyed the company of Gemma and Lucy. And that scared her more than anything.

CHAPTER TEN

"*H*ave you returned your reply card for Marie O'Keefe's wedding?" Patrick's mother asked when he arrived the following morning to drop off Lucy.

"Not yet," he said, trying to keep the irritation out of his voice. He was plenty busy enough with working and raising two girls without having to worry about getting his reply card back for his cousin's wedding.

"Margaret rang me last night and said they need the final count," his mother pressed, referring to her sister. "And they want to know if you want beef, salmon, or lamb."

Patrick lifted Lucy out of her car seat and handed her to Ada. She was half-awake. All that kite flying had worn the girls out.

"I told her you'll be bringing someone," she said.

Patrick stopped and stared at his mother. "You did what?"

She appeared nonplussed. "It's time to start moving on with your life. I know what happened with Maureen was tragic, and it was, but you're still young."

Patrick bit his tongue. "Ma, I'll move on when I'm ready."

Ada shrugged, holding Lucy, whose head rested on her shoulder. "You can take Edel. I've already told her that you would."

83

Patrick glared at his mother, his face reddening. "How dare you do that to Edel! You keep leading her on, when I have no interest. She will only end up getting hurt because of your interference. Let it go."

Ada looked wounded. "But—"

He interrupted her before she could wage her war any more, saying the first thing that popped into his head. "I've already asked someone to go with me."

His mother's eyes widened. "You have? Who?"

"Caroline," he blurted.

"Caroline?" she repeated, frowning. Her face relaxed with the slow dawning of realization. "That American?"

He nodded, immediately regretting lying to his mother and dragging Caroline into it. But she would be gone back to America by the time the wedding rolled around at the end of the month, and he'd have an out. Neither woman would ever have to know.

"I didn't realize you two were getting close," Ada said.

"We aren't getting close," he corrected. Although talking to her the night before had been cathartic. "I just asked her, that's all. Don't read too much into it."

"It's hard not to," she said. Lucy made moves to get down, and Ada set her on the ground. "Go on in, Lucy. I've got your breakfast on the table." After her granddaughter disappeared into the house, she said to Patrick, "Just be careful. You're still vulnerable. Don't let her take advantage of you."

Patrick snorted in frustration, throwing his hands up in resignation. "Ma, make up your mind. First you tell me to move on with my life, and now you're telling me to proceed with caution. Which one is it?"

"I just want you to be happy," she said.

"For right now, I'm okay, and someday I will be happy again. But please don't try to set me up with anyone. *If* I decide to move on, I'll pick her myself."

His mother's expression became pinched.

"I've got to get to work," he muttered, and he climbed into his work van. Over his shoulder, he said, "Tell Aunt Margaret I'm bringing someone, and we'll both have the beef."

CAROLINE WAS out front when Patrick pulled up several minutes later. He pushed the thought that he had just landed her in it, way out of his mind. She was leaving in a week, and he'd figure out some excuse for his mother as to why she wasn't accompanying him to the wedding. He hated weddings. They reminded him of his own: happy and so full of promise. But he was fond of his cousin Marie, and he wouldn't let her down.

Patrick pulled into the driveway behind Caroline's rental car. She waved and he smiled in return. When he'd told her about Maureen, he'd felt a relief. It was always like that. To say it out loud and have someone else hear it made it a tiny bit less painful each time. In the beginning, he couldn't tell the story without breaking down. That was the first year. Then he was able to tell the story with just tears in his eyes. Lately, when he told it, a lump formed in his throat and he felt sad, but he was able to share most of the details without his voice shaking.

He took in her bare arms in the sleeveless top. Her hair was up in a ponytail and he imagined it loose, down around her shoulders. Alarmed, he pushed those kinds of thoughts far from his mind. That's the last thing he needed: to get involved with her. He wasn't ready, he told himself.

She was smiling when he reached her.

"How's it going?" he asked.

"Fine," she said.

Patrick handed her a handful of paint palettes. "I picked these up for you so you can choose your colors. Just mark them and I'll pick up the paint."

Caroline smiled. "That's great, thanks." She glanced around. "It's another gorgeous day."

"It is," he agreed, looking around at the beach and ocean spread out before them. He looked anywhere but at her. Or her hair. Or the soft skin of her arms.

"I thought it rained here all the time," she said.

"Oh, it does. This weather is an anomaly, I assure you," he said. "There have been days here in the summer where we've had to wear our winter coats down on the beach."

Caroline laughed. "That's not right. But I suppose it's still beautiful even in the rain," she said.

He nodded. "It is." An image of her in a dress at the wedding with him floated before his eyes. His head snapped up and he said, "I'd better get to work before the day slips away from us."

"Oh, sure," she said.

Before he entered the house, she asked, "Do you live around here?"

He turned and pointed to his house, just above hers. Only the roofline was visible. She tipped her head to the side and considered this. "Wow, I didn't realize you were that close."

"I am," he said.

"We're neighbors, then, right?" she asked, her eyes studying his face. He wondered if she liked what she saw.

"That's right, we are."

"Huh, you never said."

For a moment, he stared at her, but he realized he had no reason to linger outside with her, and went into the house.

THE GIRLS WERE sound asleep in their beds later that evening.

After he picked up the bit of toys scattered around the living room, Patrick made Gemma's lunch for the next day and pressed her school uniform. But despite all these before-bedtime tasks, his thoughts kept drifting back to Caroline.

He sighed, torn. On one hand, he wanted to run his fingers through her blonde hair to see if it was as soft as it appeared. On the other hand, he wanted to bury his head in his hands and cry out. How could he be interested in someone other than Maureen, the mother of his children? Finished with his tasks, he plopped down on the sofa. He kicked off his shoes, put his feet up on the coffee table, and gazed out at the Atlantic Ocean. His heart felt heavy.

He and Maureen had had so many plans. It seemed disrespectful of him to be looking at another woman and thinking all those thoughts he had been thinking. He wondered what it would feel like to kiss Caroline. He knew by heart every detail of her arms and hands and fingers, and wondered what it would feel like to have those arms wrapped around him. She was beautiful, with curves that didn't quit. He closed his eyes at the thought of holding her in his arms. He couldn't understand what was going on. He had never fallen for anyone since Maureen. And he hadn't planned on it either, but there he was, not being able to get another woman off his mind. He sat there, just staring, looking at nothing in particular, hoping the answers would present themselves. But they never did, and he ended up falling asleep on the sofa again.

By morning, he felt slightly better. Not hopeful but no longer agitated. He drove Gemma down to her primary school, parked the car, and walked her to the school gate. There was a collection of mothers at the school gate, and their murmurings and laughter filled the morning air. He nodded at them in acknowledgement and was aware that their conversation had drifted off as he walked by. After Maureen had died, the other mothers had been very good to him, dropping off meals and picking up Gemma for play-dates so some kind of normalcy could go on despite him not wanting it to. But he had never been the type to hang out at the school gate for a chin-wag. Come to think of it, he didn't think Maureen would have been that type either. Luckily, the other mothers didn't hold it against him, and Gemma was still invited to birthday parties and playdates, which he made sure she never missed. But at times, he caught the look of pity on some of their faces, and he almost resented them for it. He was not someone to be pitied. Yes, what had happened was awful, but he didn't want or need pity.

Caroline's car was parked out front of the Burke place. She always left the loose gravel driveway empty for him, which he found thoughtful. The front door of the house was open. As he unloaded his van, he whistled absentmindedly.

"Will I help you carry something in?" Caroline asked, glancing over at all his gear.

Sheepishly, he turned toward her, thinking that her blonde hair reminded him of sunshine on a warm summer's day. Her blue eyes reminded him of bluebells that grew wild. Blushing, he scratched the back of his neck.

He shook his head. "Nah, I've got it." He followed her into the house. From behind, he had a great view of her hourglass figure in her T-shirt and capri pants. Everything on her curved. He wondered how those curves would feel under his hands.

CHAPTER ELEVEN

At breakfast the following morning, Caroline was ravenous. And tired. Since she'd met Patrick and his daughters flying kites, she hadn't had a good night's sleep. They had dominated her thoughts. The fact that he had two young daughters should definitely have dampened her desire and attraction to Patrick. But it hadn't, and that scared her.

Breda, wearing an apron with an image of the Eiffel Tower on it, set a steaming white china pot of tea on Caroline's table. With a broad smile, she said, "I didn't know you were the one who inherited Maeve Burke's property. How on earth did you know her?"

Caroline decided it was best to keep it simple. "We became friends."

"And Patrick Kelly is working on the reno of the property!" Breda made no move to walk away, despite the fact that all the other tables were full. In the background, while Breda chatted with Caroline, Joe dashed from table to table, delivering tea, plates of breakfast, and racks of toast.

Breda shook her head and tutted. "What happened to his wife

was just terrible. Having to raise those young girls all by himself."

"It was," Caroline agreed.

Breda gazed out the window as if something had caught her attention, but her expression looked as if she was far away. "It happened to me as well."

Caroline looked up quizzically at her.

Breda explained, "My first husband pulled into the passageway of our farm one day, but didn't come into the house. I wondered, 'What in the name of God is taking him so long to come inside?'" She shook her head again. "I went out and saw the car door open and Martin thrown down on the ground. It gave me quite a fright. I called the doctor straightaway, but Martin was gone. Brain aneurysm, they said. He wasn't even thirty. We'd been married for a year." She laid her hand across her chest, fingers splayed.

"I'm so sorry," Caroline said.

Breda looked at Caroline as if she'd forgotten she was there, and shrugged. "It was awful at the time. I'd been a city girl from Limerick, and suddenly I was a widow out in a rural area with a farm. I ended up selling the farm to Martin's brother—I'd no notion of milking cows—and I came down to Inch, bought this place, and started the B & B." She glanced over at Joe and smiled. "Ten years ago, I married my butcher." She caught Joe's eye and he favored her with a grin, almost as if he knew what she was talking about.

Caroline smiled. That was the kind of story she liked: the ones with happy endings.

"I'd better get back to work. Love doesn't fry up the eggs." Breda laughed and breezed out of the dining room.

~

"I CAN TAKE those down for you if you want," Patrick said, standing in the doorway wearing a white T-shirt and a pair of jeans.

Caroline frowned. "That's all right, I can do it." She'd started removing the upper cabinet doors for refinishing.

"Okay, but if you change your mind, let me know," he said, lingering in the doorway.

With a screwdriver in one hand and standing on a stepladder, Caroline removed another door. Nervously aware of his eyes on her, she lost her grip on the wooden door and it slipped out of her grasp, its metal hinges sliding down her arm and tearing at the skin as it went. Dropping the screwdriver, Caroline bit her tongue and squeezed her eyes shut.

Patrick was at her side in two strides. "Are you all right?" Putting his hand around her waist, he helped her off the stepladder as she cradled her left arm.

She extended her arm to survey the damage. There was a long, jagged cut on the inside of her forearm. Blood slid off her arm and dripped onto the floor.

Caroline turned on the tap and held her arm under the warm water. The blood made it look worse than it was.

Patrick stood beside her. "Will I take you to the GP for stitches? You might need a tetanus shot. Those hinges are old."

Caroline shook her head. "No, it's a clean cut. Not deep enough for stitches. And I had a tetanus shot two years ago."

Without a word, Patrick reached both hands into the sink and supported her injured arm as the water from the faucet sluiced over it. Caroline's breath caught when he took her arm in his hands. When he turned the tap off, blood immediately reappeared at the surface of the cut. He looked around. "I've got nothing here to use as a compress."

"I can go back to the B & B," she suggested.

"Nope, I'll drive you over to my house. I've got a first aid kit there."

She held up her bleeding arm. "I don't want to get blood all over the inside of your van."

"Oh, right." He shrugged and removed his T-shirt.

Caroline was unable to hide her surprise.

"It's clean. I just put it on this morning," he said, seeing her expression.

It wasn't that. It could have been dirty and torn and she wouldn't have noticed it. Or cared. She was having a hard time averting her eyes from his bare chest. She closed her eyes and swallowed hard. *Good Lord, give me strength.*

He folded his T-shirt in half and wrapped it around her arm. His naked torso right next to her, his delicious maleness, made her knees weak. She leaned against the sink for support. She barely suppressed a groan.

"Are you all right? You've gone a little pale," he observed.

She looked up at him. The concern in his eyes. She forced her gaze away from his anatomy. "Just felt a little dizzy."

"Come on, let's go to my house," he said. "We'll bandage you up, and I've got to get a new T-shirt. Can't walk around all day like this." He laughed.

"No, you can't," Caroline said. *Because I wouldn't get any work done.*

With her good arm guarding the injured one, she followed him out to his van. The combination of his fine physique on naked display, coupled with his concern for her, made her jittery, as if she'd consumed twenty cups of coffee. Her heart rate sped at an uncomfortable rate.

"How are the girls?" she asked once they were inside the van. She needed to distract herself. She tried to belt herself in, but it was difficult with one arm.

"Here, let me do that," he said, reaching over her, his bare chest in her personal space. She held her breath and blushed, hoping he didn't notice.

"The girls are fine," he said. He started the engine and pulled the van out onto the road.

"Do they go to school?" her voice squeaked. She coughed to clear her throat.

"Gemma is in senior infants at the primary school, and Lucy goes to my mother's house for the day."

"It must be difficult raising them by yourself," she said softly.

"It is, but I'm managing," he said. "When Maureen died, I didn't have a clue. All of the sudden, I had a two-year-old and a newborn, and no wife beside me. To be honest, I don't know how I would have done it all without the help of my mother and sister. But we've gotten this far, and we'll get by."

They pulled into his driveway. His house was a newer-build stone bungalow. It had enormous windows in the front, which afforded a great view of the beach below, something she never tired of looking at. Gingerly, she got out of his van. She followed him through the front door of his home.

She looked around the place. The tiled hall floor led to a kitchen in the back. The walls were painted various shades of aqua or blue and trimmed with white woodwork. A quick glimpse of the sitting room as she followed him back to the kitchen revealed a hardwood floor, cloth furniture, and a big-screen TV.

"What about you? Are you married? Any kids?" he asked over his shoulder.

"No. And no," she said.

When he didn't say anything she added, "I was in a long-term relationship with someone, but it didn't work out. Personal choice not to have kids."

"This personal choice, is it because you don't like children?"

She flinched. That was the last thing she wanted him to think. She'd never spent any time with children, not long enough to form an opinion. Especially an opinion of dislike. "No, not at all." She hesitated as they stepped into the kitchen. It was bright and airy with white, glossy, contemporary cabinets, an island with seating, and a table on the other side of the room. It was relatively neat considering he was a single parent.

"I'm sorry. I didn't mean to pry," he said. "Let me grab the first aid kit."

He disappeared into a utility room off the kitchen and returned with a red plastic case. They stood at the sink and he slowly removed the T-shirt and placed her arm under the tap.

Caroline wished he'd put on a shirt. She'd wait and risk bleeding to death for him to do it.

"So, you're one of those women who are focusing on your career instead of motherhood."

"No, it's not that." With a need to clarify his perception of her and a nervous laugh, she said, "I never had a desire to have children, because my own parents weren't good examples of how parenting should be. I wouldn't want to pass their parenting style onto some unsuspecting kid." There was no bitterness in her voice. She'd forgiven them a long time ago. Even before they died from the long-term effects of alcohol. Her parents hadn't been abusive, but they'd been emotionally absent.

"Oh, I don't know. You seem to have turned out all right."

She smiled. "I have my grandmother to thank for that. She provided stability and encouragement in my life when there was none."

Patrick nodded and pulled out some antiseptic. "This is going to sting."

"I know."

He poured antiseptic down along the cut, and Caroline winced. When he was finished, he cleaned it up gently with gauze. Caroline stared, hypnotized, as he held her arm in his big, calloused hand. His long, thick fingers gently dabbed excess antiseptic away. His gentleness was incongruent with his rugged physique. He pulled heavy bandages from the kit, peeled off their backing, and laid them over the cut. Caroline's eyes went back and forth between his face, which had a look of intensity as if this were the most important thing he'd ever done in his life, and his hands and fingers as they expertly dressed her wound.

When he was finished, she swallowed and said quietly, "You'd make a good nurse."

"Patrick, are you home?" called out a voice from the front of the house.

"I'm in the kitchen, Ma," he answered.

Patrick's mother arrived in the doorway, holding Lucy's hand. Ada's eyes traveled from Patrick's bare chest to Caroline and then back to her son.

"Patrick, where is your shirt?" she asked.

"Caroline cut herself and I had to use it to stop the bleeding," he said.

"Does she need to go to the GP?" Ada asked.

Caroline hated being spoken of in the third person like she wasn't there. Or didn't matter. She'd been made to feel invisible as a child. "No, I'm fine." She held up her bandaged arm as proof. "It's all set."

"Well, that's good."

"I need to get a shirt," Patrick said, disappearing from the kitchen.

Caroline stepped forward and said, "I'm Caroline Egan."

"Ada Kelly." Patrick's mother said with a nod of acknowledgement.

Lucy hung onto her grandmother's leg and smiled shyly. Caroline returned the smile.

"How are you, Lucy?" she asked.

"Have you met the children?" Ada asked, frowning.

"I have," Caroline replied, then added quickly, "On the beach."

Patrick re-entered the kitchen wearing a clean white T-shirt. Lucy ran to him and he lifted her up.

"How did you know Maeve Burke?" Ada asked. "We were all surprised when we heard she'd left her property to an American."

Caroline laughed nervously. "Not as surprised as I was. I was Maeve's nurse while she was in hospice."

Caroline immediately realized how it sounded, and the expression on Mrs. Kelly's face confirmed her suspicion. It would be useless to try and convince people that she hadn't done anything wrong or had any undue influence on the woman, even though she'd been just as surprised as everybody else when she learned of the inheritance.

"I see," was Ada's response.

"Have you had lunch?" Patrick asked Lucy, and Caroline was grateful for the change of subject.

Lucy nodded and Ada added, "We've just come from our dinner. She ate all of hers; she's been a good girl. We're heading to town to do some shopping." She turned her attention back to Caroline. "So you're planning on selling the Burke place?"

Caroline nodded. "I am. My life is in the States, and I have no plans to move here."

"There's a rumor going around that OHG group is interested in acquiring the property for holiday homes."

Caroline hesitated and finally said, "They have approached me, but I doubt they're serious."

"Oh, they'd be serious all right, they've been trying to get a property here for years," Patrick said.

"That would be a pity, wouldn't it?" Ada asked, speaking more to Patrick than to Caroline.

Caroline opened her mouth but then closed it, choosing to remain silent.

Ada changed the subject. "Egan is an Irish surname. Ancestors come from here?"

Caroline nodded. "Yes, my grandfather was born in Cork but emigrated as a young boy with his mother."

"That's interesting, so you're not that far removed."

Caroline laughed nervously. "I guess not."

"It entitles you to Irish citizenship," Ada said.

Caroline frowned, not comprehending. "I'm sorry?"

"If you have one parent or grandparent who was born in the Republic, you can become an Irish citizen. Passport and all," Ada explained.

"That wouldn't be necessary," Caroline said. "As I've said, I've no permanent plans. It just so happened that I inherited a piece of property here."

Ada rewarded her with a tight smile. "Yes, it seems some people just have all the luck."

There was an awkward silence until finally, Ada broke it. "Lucy, we'd better get on the road." She held out her arms to her granddaughter. They said their goodbyes, and Ada called over her shoulder on her way out, "We'll see you at the wedding, Caroline."

Confused, Caroline looked to Patrick, whose face had gone red.

"Would you like some lunch?" Patrick asked hurriedly. "While we're here we could have a sandwich and a cup of tea."

"That sounds great," she said. She was beginning to tire of the selection at the petrol station.

"I've got some ham, chicken, or egg mayonnaise," he said, bending down in front of the fridge.

"Ham is fine," she said. "Do you need any help?"

"Nah, sit down," he said. He turned on the kettle and while he waited for the water to boil, he made up two sandwiches for them with all the trimmings, whistling all the while.

They made small talk as they ate. Patrick talked about his girls, and Caroline talked about her life in the States and her plan to go back to college in the fall for an advanced nursing degree.

After they finished their sandwiches, Patrick brought over an apple pie and cut two slices, plated them up, and handed one to Caroline.

"What do you like to do in your spare time?" he asked.

"When I'm not working, I like hanging out with my friends. I do a bit of gardening and I love garage and estate sales," she said. "But once I start school, there probably won't be any time for any hobbies."

"Ambitious," he said in a neutral tone.

Caroline shrugged and finished her pie. "Have you always wanted to be a carpenter?"

He nodded. "Like since I was five."

Caroline thought it was wonderful when people could work jobs or have careers in fields they loved.

They ate pie in companionable silence.

Patrick drained the last of his tea and clapped his hands, the noise startling her in the stillness that had fallen between them. "We'd better get back to work. Or maybe you should take the rest of the day off."

Caroline drew in a deep breath and shook her head, trying to get her bearings back. "No, I don't need to take time off."

"Suit yourself," he said, shrugging. The atmosphere between them changed. The charge had disappeared. He nodded toward her arm. "There's no more bandages in the kit, so you might want to go to the chemist and get yourself some more."

"I will, later."

Without another word, he turned and left the room, whistling as he went, leaving Caroline staring at the empty space he left behind.

CAROLINE WOULD HAVE LOVED nothing more than to laze on the beach or even take a quick walk along the sand, she thought as she took in the magnificent view that afternoon, but she put her head down and focused on the task at hand.

Patrick had removed the remaining cabinet doors and lined them up outside. He'd set up his electric sander for her, attaching an extension cord that ran into the house.

With dust flying everywhere and the noise of the sander blocking out all other sound, she had not heard Patrick step up behind her. She jumped, startled, when she realized he was there.

"Sorry," he said, "I thought you heard me." He handed her a bottle of water. "Drink? It's hot this afternoon. The sun is splitting the rocks."

She smiled at the expression and gratefully accepted the water, uncapping it and taking a drink. It was hot but not unbearable.

Up close, she noticed he needed a shave. She'd bet his face would feel like sandpaper, and she wondered how it would feel against her skin.

"But even when it's overcast and raining, it's still a beautiful place," he said. He leaned against the makeshift workbench with a satisfied smile on his face.

Looking around, Caroline agreed with him. No matter the weather, it was most likely always beautiful.

They were interrupted by the arrival of a car, kicking gravel stones out of its way as it pulled up in front of the property. Caroline looked over to see that it was Paul Moloney from OHG. She resented him for spoiling their idyll. Apparently, Patrick did too, because he visibly stiffened and straightened up.

"I'd better get back to work," he said, and without another look at her, he headed back into the cottage.

"Ah, Caroline, I thought I'd find you here!" Paul called out with a wave as he stepped out of his car.

As he approached, he said, "How's it coming along?" He glanced at the cottage. In one hand, he held a folder, and Caroline could see the letters OHG stamped in white over a navy background.

She looked back at the house. "It's coming, slowly but surely."

"What happened to your arm?" he asked with a nod to her bandaged limb.

"Just a cut."

"When are you scheduled to return to the US?" he asked, looking at her.

"Next Wednesday," she replied.

"Less than a week. Time flies and all that."

"It sure does," she agreed.

"I've brought an offer from OHG for your property, Caroline," he said, handing her the folder.

She accepted it but didn't open it. "That was very fast, Paul."

"Well, we don't like to waste time." He smiled. "Take a look at it, think about it, and get back to me."

Caroline knew she needed to sell the property, and here was an offer that had just fallen into her lap. And she knew it would be generous. She could sell, get her cash, head back home, and move on with her life: buy Kevin out of his half of the house and pay for college. Then why wasn't she happier? Relieved? She swallowed hard at the disconnect. She didn't want to look too closely at her reason for hesitating.

From inside the house, she could hear whistling. Some Irish tune she was not familiar with, but even so, it tugged at her heart.

Him. He was the reason. He was the cause of her hesitation.

Quietly, she said, "Thank you, Paul. I will think about it. And have an answer for you soon."

"Fair enough," he said. He went on to make small talk for a few minutes but Caroline couldn't focus, her mind drifting to the man inside the cottage, whistling a lonely tune.

It was an early night for Caroline. She didn't leave the Burke place until after eight. As she was leaving, she could see faint lights coming from Patrick's bungalow. It was probably bedtime in the Kelly household. She imagined it was difficult being a single parent, but he seemed to be holding it all together.

Thoughts of Patrick nagged at her like a stiff tag on a shirt collar.

Caroline sat on the edge of her bed in her room at the B & B and did not bother to remove her jacket or her shoes.

She thought of herself as immensely practical and sensible. Dependable. Boring even. She paid her bills on time. She always voted. She always told the truth even if it was difficult. She kept her promises and did things for people that she said she would.

She walked over to her window and stared out at the ocean. The color of it reminded her of Patrick's eyes. *Stop it!* She wasn't there for romance. No way. She wasn't getting involved with anyone or anything while she was there.

But Patrick Kelly would end up being her undoing. She felt like she was back in high school, a freshman crushing on a cute senior. What scared her was that she might do something crazy and unpredictable and send her ordered life into a tailspin.

Eventually, she sank onto the bed, determined not to get pulled under by the weight of her crush on Patrick. She rationalized it. He was foreign. He had an accent. He was hot. And she was just coming off of being dumped. It was almost like a perfect alignment of the planets, except it was going to end up wrecking her head. And her heart.

The image of him with his girls on the beach the other night was just what she thought she needed. It should have been a bucket of cold water putting out a very hot fire. But when the thought of his two lovely daughters came to mind and how she'd enjoyed their company it did not have its intended effect of stifling her desire for Patrick.

She found Breda and managed to borrow some cling wrap to wrap her arm so she could take a shower. Afterward, in her pajamas and with a towel wrapped around her head like a turban, she sat on the bed and booted up her laptop. In her inbox was a letter from the college. It was a list of requirements and her schedule for the fall semester.

When she was finished looking at that, she felt still awake. She sat on the bed with a pillow behind her, leaning against the headboard with her legs stretched out. She pulled the OHG folder to her and opened it up on her lap. She studied the paperwork inside and their generous offer.

CHAPTER TWELVE

$\mathcal{P}$atrick was grateful for the weekend away from the Burke place and more especially, from Caroline. The American woman was beginning to dominate his thoughts, and that had to stop. Fortunately, she was due to return to the States midweek, and then he could stop this nonsense. Stop thinking about her.

It was Father's Day, and his plan was to make a big breakfast and then spend the day with the girls at the beach.

There was a knock at the front door. "Gemma, see who's at the door," he said. He stood at the stove making pancakes, scrambled eggs, sausages, and rashers.

"Is your Dad home?" a female voice asked. It sounded like Caroline, but she wouldn't be here on Sunday. Would she?

Gemma bolted back down the hall, shouting, "Daddy! It's Caroline!"

Patrick turned down the burner on the stove and set the spatula on a plate.

Caroline stood on the doorstep, looking around. Like her property, his commanded an incredible view of Inch Strand and

Macgillicuddy's Reeks across the inlet. A short, dense hedge boxed the perimeter of the property. A pink bike lay on its side on the grass.

Patrick was unable to hide the surprise on his face.

"Caroline!" he said.

"Look, I'm sorry to bother you, but I wanted to run something by you."

"Of course," he said. He threw open the door and with a nod of his head, he said, "Come in." He knew she wouldn't bother him at home unless it was something important.

Hesitantly, she stepped inside and followed him back to the open-plan kitchen, which looked out over the back garden and the golden-brown scrub of the Dingle mountains. There was a swing set and a trampoline in the backyard.

He followed her stare as her eyes landed on the kitchen table, set with three place settings: one regular plate and two smaller melamine plates, one in pink and one in yellow. Lucy sat in a booster seat on a chair, wearing a bib and waiting patiently for her breakfast.

Caroline pulled up short. "Oh, I'm sorry, I didn't mean to interrupt your breakfast."

"No worries," he said, returning to the stove to turn the eggs. He removed the rashers and sausages from the grill and laid them on a paper towel on a plate. The electric kettle steamed on the countertop and clicked off. He put bread into the toaster.

"It's Father's Day," Gemma announced. "And we're going to the beach today. And Daddy said if we're good, we can get ice cream."

"I didn't realize it was Father's Day . . ." Caroline began, then changed her mind and turned to go. "I shouldn't have come. I'm sorry. I'll see you in the morning."

"Caroline, wait," he said, reaching out and taking hold of her arm. He lowered his voice. "You don't have to leave."

Again she hesitated, her mouth opening and then closing, no words coming forth.

"Have some breakfast," he said. He indicated that she should sit down at the table.

She shook her head. "No, thanks. I've eaten. But please, don't let me interrupt yours."

"At least have a cup of tea," he said.

"Tea would be nice," she agreed.

He plated up the girls' breakfasts and laid them in front of them. He made two mugs of tea and set them down on the table. The toast popped up and he set about buttering it.

"Do you need some help?" she asked.

"Nah, everything is under control." He smiled. He nodded toward the table. "Sit down and fix your tea."

Once everyone was all set, he sat down and forked scrambled eggs into his mouth.

"When I went to the house this morning, I found two puddles of water on the floor," Caroline said.

"Really?" he asked.

"In the corner in the kitchen and on the other side of the wall in the bedroom," she explained, sipping at her tea.

He frowned as he leaned over and cut up Gemma's sausage. With his fork, he tapped her plate. "Come on, love, start eating."

Caroline waited as Patrick chewed thoughtfully. "Let me finish up here and we'll go take a look at it."

Caroline's eyes widened. "I think it can wait until tomorrow."

"Best to take a look at it," he said, shoveling more food into his mouth. "Girls, eat up, we've got to go to Caroline's." He looked quickly at her. "Is it okay that I bring them along?"

"Of course it is," she replied.

Patrick explained he'd follow Caroline back to the cottage because it would be too much of a hassle transferring the girls' car seats to her car. She pulled out of his yard with him behind her.

In less than three minutes, they were back at the Burke place. She led him through to the kitchen. Her eyes widened. "It's much bigger than it was before."

Patrick set down Lucy, and the two girls ran off to explore the rest of the rooms.

"Don't touch anything," Patrick called out after them.

He squatted and inspected the puddle. This was not good.

He stood up and walked to the other room to examine the water on the floor in there. "There's a leak, obviously. Coming from one of the pipes beneath the floor," he told Caroline when he returned to the kitchen.

Caroline groaned. "That sounds expensive."

Patrick nodded. "Yeah. The floor is going to have to be ripped up, down to the foundation. The house is old, and the pipes are most likely original. We'll need to ring a plumber."

"Do you know someone?" she asked.

"I do. I know a couple, actually. As it's a Sunday and it's not an emergency, I'll give them a ring first thing in the morning," he said. "In the meantime, let me shut of the water valve so the place doesn't end up flooded."

"I'm supposed to head back to the States on Wednesday," she said.

With his hands on his hips, he regarded her. "Look, if you can't stay on, I can handle it and contact you with any more issues."

"Okay."

He could tell that she was worried. Her frown said it all. Her inheritance was turning into a challenge. An expensive one. He turned off the valve to the water supply.

"I'll be here early in the morning," he said. "Girls!" he called. The girls came running, breathless, and stood by their father. "Time to go."

"We're going to the beach and then we're going for ice cream, Caroline. Do you want to come with us?" Gemma asked.

Caroline smiled. "No, thank you."

"Are you sure?" Patrick asked. He knew it was dangerous to spend any more time with her than he already was, but he couldn't seem to help himself. "Do you have something against ice cream?"

She laughed. "No, it's just that I want to get the cabinet doors finished. I stained them yesterday and was hoping to put a sealant on them today."

He smirked. "On a Sunday?"

"Well, all right then," she said with a laugh. "You've twisted my arm."

She should laugh more often, he thought. It made her look even more beautiful than she already was.

PATRICK AND CAROLINE sat on a blanket on the beach. Patrick sprayed sunscreen onto Gemma. When Lucy appeared to be struggling with undoing the buckle of her sandal, Caroline offered to help. The young girl thrust her foot into Caroline's lap, causing Caroline to burst out laughing. Once the sandals were unbuckled, Caroline set them aside onto the corner of the blanket.

"Remember, girls, no walking across the blanket. We don't want sand everywhere," Patrick said.

"But there's already sand everywhere," Gemma observed, looking around at the beach.

Caroline laughed at his daughter's obvious observation.

"Don't encourage her behavior, Caroline," he joked. Lowering his voice, he admitted, "It really becomes a game of who can outsmart the other."

Caroline grinned, and Patrick's smile lit up his face.

Patrick stripped down to his swim trunks, turned to Caroline, and saw that her eyes were on him. "Do you not have a bathing costume, Caroline?" He'd like to see her in one.

"No, I didn't think to bring one with me from the States," she said. "The thought of swimming never crossed my mind."

Patrick and the girls began filling the pails with sand to make a sandcastle. He looked over at her and said with a nod of his head, "Come on, Caroline, give us a hand."

As the four of them worked on building a castle and a moat, an older couple walked by, and they nodded in acknowledgement. The elderly woman said to Caroline with a smile, "You have a beautiful family."

After she walked away, Caroline and Patrick looked at each other and grinned.

Once the sandcastle and moat were finished, they took the girls into the water. Caroline rolled up the legs of her capris and waded into the surf up to her knees. Patrick took Gemma and Lucy further out and after about an hour, when he recognized the signs that the girls were beginning to tire, they headed to shore and back to their blanket.

Patrick dried his body with a striped beach towel. Caroline searched through their bag, helping the girls to a snack. Once the snacks were distributed, Caroline sat back and dug her heels into the sand.

"You look deep in thought, Caroline," Patrick said, standing at the edge of the beach blanket and staring down at her.

Looking up at him, she shielded her eyes from the sun. "Do I?"

He sat next to her on the blanket, his damp arm brushing against hers.

Gemma handed Patrick her juice box, and he took the straw out of the wrapper, poked it through the box, and gave it back. In turn, Lucy handed Caroline her own juice box. Caroline readied it for her and handed it back.

"You know, you have a natural way with kids," he observed.

Caroline responded with a sharp laugh. "Why? Because I can manage to get a straw into a juice box? Seriously, I don't have a clue about kids," she admitted.

"None of us do," he said. "It's not like they come with instruction manuals."

She looked at him, digging her toes into the warm sand.

He continued. "You should have seen me trying to change a diaper for the first time. I didn't know which end was up. And whenever I changed their clothes, I always managed to get something from the dressing table underneath their shirts. A tube of diaper cream, a baby comb," he said with a laugh.

"Everything but the kitchen sink?" Caroline laughed.

"Just about," Patrick concurred.

"I'd be so afraid I'd screw them up," Caroline admitted, staring at the water.

"You said your parents had some problems, and yet look how well you turned out," he pointed out.

She drew her knees up and hugged them. "I don't know. I never had the desire to have children."

"Even when you were with your partner?" he questioned.

"I just don't think I'd be any good at it."

He didn't judge her on this, because there was nothing to judge. It was none of his business. Patrick looked over at his daughters, who sat ten feet in front of them in the sand, drinking from their juice boxes and chatting amongst themselves.

"What do you think is the most desirable trait for a nurse to possess?" he asked Caroline.

Caroline replied right away. "To simply care for the other person is the base to start with."

"Parenting isn't much different."

He knew she was going home in a few days. And that was a good thing. Because he was starting to have feelings for her that scared the life out of him.

CHAPTER THIRTEEN

On Monday morning, Caroline was there early, before Patrick or the plumber. There was no sun that day, just gray skies to match Caroline's mood. She sat down on the step stool in the hall, looking in at the water-covered floor, and said, "Ugh," to no one in particular. This inheritance was pricey. The thing she feared most was what it was turning into: a money pit.

She heard the front door open behind her and knew by the familiar tread that Patrick had arrived. He leaned against the kitchen doorframe with one muscular arm and let out a low whistle.

"At least it hasn't gotten worse," Patrick pointed out.

Caroline sighed. She wasn't up for any more surprises that cost money.

"Cheer up, it could be worse," he said, trying and failing to lift her spirits.

"I don't see how."

A cloud passed over his face. "Trust me, there are worse things than this."

Caroline lowered her head, embarrassed. In the whole scheme of things, this wasn't that important, more a headache and an inconvenience than anything else. "Of course, you're right. I'm sorry."

Patrick looked sheepish. "I wasn't drawing on any specific life experiences of my own," he said. "It just happens to be my point of view. I tend to look at the positive."

Before she could reply, there was a sharp rap at the front door.

"Hello?" someone called out.

Caroline and Patrick stepped forward together and pushed up against each other, each looking at the other and muttering, "Sorry." Patrick held out his hand and said, "Ladies first."

Frowning at him, Caroline said, "Gee, thanks."

The plumber, a middle-aged man named Charley Dee, had hair the color of a carrot and was covered in freckles. He nodded, walked right past Caroline and Patrick, and waded through the thin layer of water on the kitchen floor. He stood with his hands on his hips, surveyed the room, grunted, and said, "Hmmm." He left the kitchen, headed toward the bedroom, and repeated the routine. Finally, he came back out into the hall, lifting his flat cap with his hand and scratching his forehead with his finger.

"I'll need to dig a trench in the floor to get at those pipes," he announced, his loud voice booming through the place.

"In the kitchen and the bedroom?" Caroline asked.

"Yes," the plumber replied.

Caroline's shoulders sagged. That sounded like a labor-intensive job.

She nodded. "How soon would you be able to start?"

"Not until next week or the week after," he said. "I'm all booked up."

Caroline grimaced. It would really delay things. "What about the leak and all the water on the floor?" she asked.

"Is the water shut off?" he asked Patrick.

Patrick nodded.

"You can use a shop vac to remove the water from the floor," he said.

"Can you give me a written estimate?" she asked.

"I can," he said. "I'll drop it through the letterbox in the morning."

After the plumber left, she turned to Patrick and asked, "Do you know of any other plumbers?"

Patrick stood there with his arms folded across his chest. Caroline tried not to stare at the biceps visible beneath the short sleeves of his T-shirt. Ropey veins ran the length of his arms.

"I know three other plumbers that I could recommend. But two are booked for the month and the third is away on holiday until next week."

Caroline sighed, frustrated. "I don't have time for this." She waved her arm around the kitchen indicating to all the water on the floor.

"It will get done, relax, don't worry about it."

"I know, but I have to go home," she said.

"You'll get home in time. And I can manage while you're gone," he said reassuringly.

"I suppose so," Caroline muttered. She surveyed the room. There was no sense in staring at the mess that was the kitchen floor. Not when the cabinets needed to be sealed.

"What are you doing today?" Caroline asked Patrick.

"After I get the water off the floor, I was going to start painting the front rooms," he said. She'd already picked out paint colors from the palettes he'd given her. Nice, cool pastels.

Caroline needed to get out of the house, because it was beginning to give her a major headache.

"I'm going to give those cabinet doors a quick seal and then I think I'll investigate what's out in that old shed in the back garden."

113

"Just be careful, everything is neglected back there," Patrick warned.

Tilting her head to one side, Caroline asked, "Is that your way of showing you care?"

His cheeks colored, and Caroline was glad she wasn't the only one who could be embarrassed at a little bit of flirting. He tilted his own head and said, "Maybe."

Laughing, Caroline went out the front door. Once the cabinet doors were set up, she went about applying a coat of sealant. Once she was finished, she wiped off the brush on a rag and sealed the can shut with the lid.

She headed out to the back of the property. She stood in the garden and assessed the landscaping. The grass was overgrown over most of the ten acres. There were some wild rosebushes that needed care, and a fuchsia bush that was in desperate need of a trim. But it was too much to tackle now.

She headed toward the shed at the back of the property. It was a whitewashed stone building that was long and narrow in structure. It had a low roof and low square windows. The walls and forms were uneven, suggesting it had been constructed by hand. A long time ago.

The shed door was padlocked, but the lock was rusted. Caroline tried all the keys on the ring that the solicitor had given her, but none fit.

Exhaling loudly, Caroline went to one of the windows and wiped it off with the back of her hand to peek in. Because the windows were small, the interior was dimly lit. She could see there were all sorts of things about, but except for a chair and an old dresser, she couldn't make out what the rest of the contents were. It made her more anxious to get inside and investigate. Treasures might await, she thought.

Caroline headed back inside the house and found Patrick in the front room. Blue painter's tape skirted around the edge of the ceiling and the baseboard. He stood on a ladder, cutting along the top of the wall with a paintbrush. A can of paint stood in the middle of the room, open, revealing the pale periwinkle color she'd chosen.

"I know you're busy, Patrick," she said, "but when you take a break, would you be able to get the padlock open? I have no key, and it's rusted over."

"Sure, no problem," he said.

"Can I open a window before the paint fumes overpower you?" she asked.

He looked at her with a grin and asked, "Afraid I might pass out?"

"Maybe," she said.

"Do you promise to nurse me back to health?" he asked.

Caroline laughed. "Back to work, Patrick. I'll be outside."

She retreated to the front steps, sat down, and stretched her legs out before her, tilting her face toward the sky. She knew she should put on her wide-brimmed sun hat, but the warmth felt so good on her face that she didn't.

Her reverie was interrupted by the An Post van pulling up out front. Frank Dolan got out of the van and lumbered up the foot-path, whistling, to where she sat on the stoop.

Frank handed her a glossy advert. "Here's some post for you."

It was a catalogue for SuperValu, the grocery chain. "Thanks, Frank."

Frank nodded toward the house. "How's it going?"

Caroline shrugged. "Not so good at the moment." She explained to him about the leak underneath the kitchen floor.

"Pay no mind to that," Frank said with a smile. "It's an old house, so there's bound to be problems. It's like people. They get old, they have problems." He looked over at the house and announced, "But it's a sound house, and it deserves a second chance."

"That's what I'm hoping for," she said. "But right now, the problems seem overwhelming and expensive."

"Ah, sure, it'll be grand," he said. "Caroline, do you know how old I am?"

Caroline grinned at the abrupt change of subject and wondered if Frank was trying to take her mind off the house. "I don't know. Maybe in your sixties?"

He laughed and slapped his thigh. "Ah go on, sixties! Sure, haven't I gone seventy-four just this last Christmas?" He paused and chuckled. "I'm from Dublin, born and reared. Worked for the postal service up there from the time I was sixteen. I was also a raging alcoholic up there—on and off the job." He shook his head. "When I was fifty, my supervisor discovered that I was only delivering one piece of post each day. The first house on my route was owned by Mad Jack Madigan, who was a bigger drunk than me. I'd deliver his post and then spend the rest of the day drinking with Mad Jack. Looking back, I suppose I should have delivered to his house last." Frank looked thoughtful.

"What happened? How did you end up here?" she asked.

"Well," he said with a laugh, "my supervisor found all the undelivered post in the back of my van. I'd been out of work for a few days on a bender. Anyway, I was passed out in my bedsit, and my supervisor showed up. I don't remember much, because I was drunk, but he packed all my things and me into his car and drove me out of Dublin. Said I'd be the death of him. Once we left County Dublin, he told me he was taking me as far away from Dublin as possible. For my own good as well as his."

"Is that how you ended up here?"

"Yes. We landed in Annascaul, which isn't too far from here. He had a sister who'd been a missionary nun for over fifty years but had returned to Ireland to live out her retirement. When he left me with his sister, he told me I was never to step foot in Dublin again, that it wasn't big enough for the two of us. It took me a year to get sober with the help of the good sister."

"Did you ever go back to Dublin?" Caroline asked.

He shook his head. "No. Never wanted to."

As he walked away, he said, "The moral of the story is, don't give up on your house, or people, just because they're old and have problems. There may still be a lot of life left in them."

Caroline thought about his story long after he left.

THE POSTMAN WASN'T GONE LONG when Patrick appeared in the doorway. "I've got all the ceilings cut in. It's the lock you want opened?"

She stood up and stumbled, but he reached for her to steady her.

"Um, thanks," she said.

Patrick grabbed a bolt cutter from the back of his van and followed Caroline to the back garden. He bent over and worked at the lock with the bolt cutter. Caroline stared at his back and wondered what it would be like to lie next to him at night, rubbing his back after a hard day's work. Or maybe just circling her arms around his waist and cuddling up to him.

The padlock snapped open and fell to the ground, startling Caroline from her thoughts. Patrick picked it up and held it out to her. "Did you want to keep it?" he asked.

She shook her head and stepped through the door, pushing thoughts of him away. The place was dark and smelled of wet earth. The ceiling was low, and she had to brush away cobwebs. Patrick was behind her. Her skin tingled with the nearness of him.

"Would you look at all this rubbish?" He snorted.

Caroline picked up an old three-legged wooden stool. In her

mind, she was already cleaning it up, sanding it, and staining it for another purpose. Maybe something to set books on?

"That's an old milking stool," Patrick said.

"I figured."

"Give it to me and I'll toss it for you," he said.

She held it closer. "You will not. I will repurpose this."

"Suit yourself."

"What are those, over there against the wall?" she asked, pointing to a pair of waist-high aluminum cans that had two handles.

"Huh, those are the old milking cans from about a hundred years ago."

Caroline could already see them out front, one on each side of the door, with flowers overflowing from them.

She looked around at the rest of the contents in the old shed. There were tools and tires and all sorts of miscellaneous items. A sense of determination and purpose filled her. There were some pieces she could salvage for the house to restore it to its former glory and rich heritage. A frisson of excitement pulsed through her.

"I hope the skip is big enough," Patrick said from behind her.

"It should be," she answered vaguely, her mind focused on sorting through the items mentally and deciding what she wanted to save. "There are some things in here I'll want to keep."

"Then I'll leave it up to you," Patrick said. He stepped out of the shed and Caroline followed him.

"You've got a gleam in your eye, Caroline," he said with a grin.

"Do I?" she asked.

He glanced to the house and back to the shed. "Uh oh. It looks like you're starting to get attached to the place."

Before she could retort, his phone rang.

Patrick glanced at the screen and frowned. "Sorry. I have to take this."

Caroline didn't want to stand there and listen in on his conversation, but he didn't move away. She began to remove the stool and the milk cans from the shed. It was hard not to overhear what was being said.

"What's wrong, Ma?" Patrick asked. He went quiet as he listened. "I'll be right there."

Patrick disconnected from the call and looked at Caroline. "It's my mother. She's having a terrible pain in her calf."

Caroline raised her eyebrows. "That needs to be checked out."

"That's what I thought," he said. "She said it's hot, as well."

"You'd better go," she advised.

He hesitated and then asked quickly, "Would you mind coming home with me? Take a look at it? I mean with you being a qualified nurse and all. Do you mind?"

"Not at all." She set the milk cans and the stool back in the shed and closed the door. She went with Patrick out to his van, and they arrived at his mother's house in under three minutes.

"Ma?" he called out.

"I'm in here," she said from the front room.

Patrick opened the door. "I've brought Caroline with me. She's a trained nurse over in the States."

Ada seemed to take no notice of Caroline. From the expression on her face, Caroline could see she was in a lot of pain. She sat on her sofa with her feet elevated on a footstool.

Lucy lay on the back of the sofa, a toy in each hand, oblivious to the drama going on around her.

"When did this start, Ma?" Patrick asked.

"Actually, last night," Ada explained. "I thought maybe I'd been on my feet too much yesterday so I went to bed early, but it was no better in the morning."

"Why didn't you tell me when I dropped Lucy off this morning?" Patrick asked.

"Because you needed to go to work," she said.

Caroline interrupted. "Mrs. Kelly, can you tell me exactly where you have the pain?"

Patrick's mother pointed to the front of her shin and the back of her calf.

"How would you describe the pain?" Caroline queried.

"My shin is throbbing, but it's a stabbing pain in my calf." Ada grimaced. "I just can't get comfortable."

"Did you take anything for it?" Caroline asked.

"I took two paracetamol."

"Did it relieve the pain at all?"

Ada shook her head. "Didn't touch it."

"May I examine your calf?" Caroline asked.

Ada nodded.

Caroline knelt down in front of the woman and felt along her calf. Mrs. Kelly's affected leg was warm to the touch in the calf area, but there were no signs of redness.

"Have you called your doctor? I think you really need to go in and see him," Caroline suggested.

"I'll ring him right now," Patrick said.

After he left the room with his phone to his ear, Ada addressed Caroline. "What do you think it is?"

Caroline shrugged. "It could be any number of things, but the new onset of acute pain is something that shouldn't be ignored."

"Yes, but what do you think it is?"

Caroline sighed. The woman was not to be denied. "Like I said, it could be a number of things. But you should see a doctor immediately to rule out the possibility of a blood clot."

Ada nodded and said, "I wondered about that."

Patrick returned and stood in the doorway. "The GP's office said to come in now."

"I can't go now," Ada said. "Who's going to mind Lucy?"

"Where's Deirdre?" he asked.

"She's gone up to Dublin. She won't be back until tomorrow."

They were all quiet for a moment until Caroline found her voice. "I can watch her."

Patrick and his mother stared at her as if she had suggested something ridiculous. They started to protest, but Caroline held up her hand. "Really, I don't mind." She ignored her rising anxiety at the thought of being alone with the child.

"All right, come on, Ma, let's get you to the GP," Patrick said, assisting his mother up off the sofa. "Lucy, I'm taking Gran to the GP. Caroline will mind you." He added sternly, "Behave yourself."

Patrick helped his mother out to the van.

"Don't give her anything to eat or drink, or she'll spoil her dinner," Ada called out. "There's a cottage pie on the cooker. Just put it in at one hundred and eighty degrees for forty-five minutes. If we're not back by one, give Lucy her dinner, please."

Caroline nodded.

Once his van disappeared from view, Caroline looked back at Lucy, who had bounced off the sofa and stood there, staring at her.

"I want a drink and a snack," the little girl announced.

Caroline blinked. Glancing at her watch, she realized it would be awhile until it was time to serve Lucy's meal.

"Your gran said you'd be eating your dinner soon," Caroline pointed out.

"But I'm hungry."

Caroline decided to try the age-old technique of distraction. "Do you like to color or play games?"

The girl nodded quickly. She jumped up and down. "I like 'I Spy!'"

"Oh, that's a good one," Caroline agreed. "Will we go out into the garden and play it?"

As soon as they arrived out back, Lucy began to jump around and said, "Okay, Caroline, you start."

Caroline looked around the back garden. Though small, there was something to look at everywhere. There was a rectangular patch on the left-hand side that was lush with a variety of vegetables. Caroline was more of a flower person, so other than the lettuce, cabbage, and carrot tops that grew, she recognized nothing else. But she did recognize the various flowers: the purple salvia, the pink pompom dahlias, the sunflowers. It was pretty. She imagined how nice it would be to sit out there in the morning with a cup of coffee.

"Come on, Caroline," Lucy urged.

Caroline scanned the environment. She hadn't a clue as to what to do with a four-year-old. What if she was too hard on her? Or too easy?

"Okay, I spy with my little eye something red," she finally said.

Lucy, stretching her arms, gave a little jump and began to look around her gran's garden in earnest.

Almost immediately, she pointed to the red geranium. "The flower."

Caroline shook her head. "Nope."

"Gran's garden gloves?"

Caroline shook her head.

Lucy scanned the garden again and yelled, "The little red fairy door!" When Caroline nodded her head, the little girl clapped her hands.

When she tired of the game, Caroline nodded toward the vegetable garden and asked, "Do you know what kind of vegetables are growing there?"

Lucy looked at them and nodded. She walked over and pointed at big, bushy plants with the beginnings of white flowers.

"Those are potatoes. Gran said when the flowers fall off, we can dig them up."

"Will you be helping her pick them?" Caroline asked.

Lucy shrugged. "Gran lets me water the garden and the flowers."

"You must be doing a very good job, because everything is so big and green," Caroline said.

It was less than an hour before Patrick arrived back with his mother.

There was a deep frown across his forehead, and his eyes darted around the room. His mother had remained in the car.

"I need to take her to the A & E over in Tralee," he said. "The GP suspects a clot."

"That's awful."

Patrick appeared to be struggling with something.

"Is there anything I can do?" Caroline asked, sensing hesitation.

"I hate to ask, but would you be able to mind the girls until I get home?" he asked. "My sister is up in Dublin and can't leave until her equine clinic is finished, and our neighbor, Edel, is away in Spain for the week."

Caroline was at a loss for words. On one hand, she wanted to help him out, but watch two children? How could she manage that? He could be gone all day.

"I wouldn't ask if I wasn't in a bind," he said.

Coming to her senses, Caroline said, "Of course not. It's no problem." How could she not help him? And how hard would it be to watch two girls? It wasn't like he was asking her to tame lions and tigers.

"I really appreciate this," he said. "One of the other mothers will drop Gemma here after school. You can either stay here or walk down to my house. The back door is open. You have my cell number and you can ring me any time with questions."

"Okay." She blinked rapidly, processing what he was saying and what she had signed up for.

Ada sat in the front seat of Patrick's car. She rolled down her window as Caroline approached with Lucy.

"Caroline, please make yourself at home," she said through a grimace. She looked pale. She turned to Lucy and smiled. "Be a good girl, Lucy."

Patrick started the car, and Caroline stepped back with Lucy and stood on the front step, watching him drive away. Lucy slipped her hand into Caroline's, and Caroline looked down at the little girl, fear flooding her as she wondered what she was supposed to do with her for the rest of the afternoon.

Lucy showed her the doorstop in the shape of a cat. Caroline could tell she was enamored with it. Then Lucy wanted to color, which was fine with Caroline. From a cupboard, Lucy pulled out a plastic box full of crayons and markers, and took out some paper. Caroline sat with her at the kitchen table, and the two of them drew and colored. She hadn't realized how relaxing coloring could be. An adult coloring book was now on her to-buy list.

While they colored, the cottage pie baked in the oven. When it was ready, Caroline removed it and set it on top of the stove. Lucy showed her where the plates and silverware were located. Caroline dished up two plates, with a smaller portion for Lucy. Steam rose from them, and Caroline set them on the counter to cool for a bit. It looked delicious: the base was a ground beef mixed with carrots and peas in a sauce, topped with mashed potatoes with a golden-brown crust.

After dinner, she and Lucy watched a Disney movie. Lucy sang along with all the songs, which Caroline found amusing.

She heard a car pull up outside and knew this to be Gemma.

Caroline and Lucy went to the front door just as Gemma was getting out of the car. The woman in the car waved and smiled at Caroline and said goodbye to Gemma.

"Hello, Gemma," Caroline greeted her. "How was school?"

Gemma rewarded her with a gap-toothed smile and asked, "Are you minding us today?"

"Yes, I am," Caroline said, and indicated to the girls that they should head into the house.

Gemma took her backpack off and laid it on the kitchen chair.

"Do you need to get changed?" Caroline asked.

Gemma nodded. "Gran keeps clothes here for us." She ran from the room. She appeared minutes later and handed Caroline her uniform. Caroline folded it neatly and placed it with the backpack.

Caroline heated up a small plate of cottage pie for Gemma and laid it in front of her with a glass of milk. The girl lowered her head and devoured what was on the plate.

When she finished, she looked up at Caroline and asked, "Can I have a sweet?"

"What would you like?" Caroline asked, wondering if that was too much of a loaded question to ask a six-year-old.

"A biscuit, please," Gemma replied. She pointed to a bread box on the counter. "Gran keeps them in there."

Caroline brought over a box of custard creams, and Gemma helped herself to two.

"Is that your favorite biscuit?" Caroline asked.

The girl shook her head. "No, bourbon creams are my favorite."

Caroline blinked and hoped it wasn't a cookie made with bourbon.

"It's chocolate. I love chocolate," Gemma said.

"Me, too. My favorite cookie—er, biscuit—is a chocolate chip cookie."

Gemma frowned, and Lucy asked, "What's a chocolate chip cookie?"

Caroline raised her eyebrows. "Have you never had a chocolate chip cookie?"

Gemma and Lucy shook their heads.

Caroline bit her lip and thought for a moment. She wasn't much of a baker, but she had a chocolate chip cookie recipe she knew by heart. "If your gran has all the ingredients, maybe we could make a batch?"

The girls grinned and said, "Yes!" and Lucy clapped her hands.

"Let's see what your gran has. Do you know where she keeps her sugar and flour?"

The girls showed her the cupboard with the sugar, flour, and spices. Caroline hoped Mrs. Kelly wouldn't mind her hijacking her kitchen. The girls helped her gather the ingredients and lay them on the table. It dawned on Caroline that it might be unlikely that Mrs. Kelly had chocolate morsels on hand, and she didn't want to let the girls down. But after rooting around in the cabinet, she found some chocolate bars, and she felt they would do. She could just break them up into pieces.

Caroline showed the girls how to sift flour and how to pack brown sugar. Gemma and Lucy were focused on their tasks, and Caroline was surprised to find the time flying. By the time she pulled the baking sheets of cookies out of the oven, it was almost five o'clock.

Lucy took one look at the crisp, golden cookies and announced, "They're yellowlicious!"

Caroline used a spatula to remove them to a cooling rack. She poured three glasses of milk and told the girls to pick two cookies each.

The three of them sat around the table, and Caroline studied the girls' expressions as they took their first bite. Warm, gooey chocolate was hard to beat.

"Well, ladies, what do you think?" she asked.

The girls enthused over them. Gemma declared them yummy,

and Lucy clapped her hands.

They were just finishing up when Patrick walked in. He took in the scene of the three of them at the kitchen table with their cookies and milk.

"What's going on here?" he asked with a smile.

"We made chocolate chip cookies with Caroline," Gemma answered.

Patrick raised his eyebrows and helped himself to a cookie off the cooling rack.

"How's your mother?" Caroline asked.

"Okay. In the right place. They're going to run some tests, but it will be awhile." He paused and looked at the cookie he'd just bitten into. "These are delicious."

Caroline felt her cheeks color. "Thank you."

"I've got to head back over to the hospital, but I wanted to check on the three of you," he said.

"Sure, of course," Caroline said. "The girls and I are doing fine."

"My sister is on her way back from Dublin and should be at the hospital in the next hour," he said. "I can't thank you enough for your help, Caroline."

"It was no problem at all," she said.

"Look, when Deirdre gets to the hospital, I'll leave and come here for you and the girls," he said.

"All right," she said. Quickly, she added, "Take your time. There's no rush."

"Girls, I've got to go back to Gran. Be good for Caroline. I'll be back in a bit. Okay?" he said. He knelt down and they ran to him. He enveloped them in a big hug, and he squeezed his eyes shut. When he stood up, he took another cookie. "I'll take one for the road."

Caroline and the girls followed him to the front door.

"Listen, Patrick, you've got your hands full, so don't bother coming to work tomorrow," she said. She could hardly expect him to show up to work with his mother in the hospital.

"We'll see," he said. He smiled. "Don't you think you'd miss my charming personality?"

Caroline chuckled. "Well, there is that. I guess I'll just have to make the sacrifice." *Oh wow*, she thought. *Am I flirting again*? She drew in a deep breath and sobered up. "Seriously, take the day off."

"I'll think about it," he said quietly.

They stood in the front hall for a moment, with Lucy hanging on Patrick's leg. It was the way he was looking at her. It felt like a warm summer breeze over bare skin. Something passed between them, something Caroline was hesitant to acknowledge.

"You'd better get back to the hospital," she said.

"Yeah, I should go," he said, and he turned and walked out the front door.

CAROLINE WAS JUST UNLOADING the last of the dishes from Mrs. Kelly's dishwasher when Patrick returned.

"Caroline, you don't have to do that," he said. "I'll get it later."

"I'm almost done, and the girls showed me where most of the stuff goes."

He was quiet. Caroline noticed the dark circles under his eyes, and thought he looked a bit pale.

"Any word on your mother?" Caroline asked. She needed neutral subjects to talk about. The flirting earlier had left her confused.

"They've done a couple of tests. She doesn't have a clot," he said, the relief evident on his face. "She has something called a dissecting Baker's cyst."

Caroline nodded. She'd heard of it before. "The symptoms of that mimic those of a blood clot."

Patrick nodded. "That's what the doctor said. They're going to aspirate the cyst, as it's leaking behind her knee. Her blood pressure has been a little high, so they're going to keep her overnight."

"All right," she said.

"Caroline, I can't thank you enough for helping us out today," he said sincerely.

"It wasn't a problem at all," Caroline said with a smile. And she meant it.

"You're probably anxious to get back to your property," he said. "Look, I know you're leaving on Wednesday, so leave the cabinet doors and I'll hang them back up. I don't want you lifting them by yourself. They're too heavy."

Caroline nodded, touched by his thoughtfulness. It was time to leave and she had to admit to being disappointed. The afternoon had flown by with the girls. It hadn't turned out to be as bad as she feared. Surprisingly, it had been quite enjoyable.

Patrick glanced over at the girls, who sat quietly on the sofa, watching television. He chuckled. "What did you do to them? They look knackered."

"We've been busy. Coloring, playing games, baking cookies. Plus, I'm a novelty."

He regarded her for a moment. "Yes, you are a novelty."

Caroline swallowed. "Look, I can walk back. It's probably less than ten minutes."

"Not a hope, Caroline," he said. "Let me drive you."

When he said her name, goosebumps broke out on her arms.

"No, if it's all the same, I'd prefer to walk," she said. The need for some exercise and fresh sea air was now crucial. With the easy flirting earlier, she'd felt a shift in their relationship, and more than anything, she wanted to clear her head.

LATER, back in her room at the B & B, she showered, then sat on the bed in a bathrobe, towel drying her hair. She thought of her day with Patrick's girls. It had gone well. They were lovely girls, and that was a reflection on Patrick. She'd realized something about herself that day. She loved taking care of people and things, whether it was through nursing or rehabbing an old house. It was something she was good at. And she had enjoyed all those things she'd done for the girls that afternoon, from making sure they were properly fed, to baking and playing games with them. Maybe her relationships with children—whether she had her own or not—didn't have to be about how she herself was raised, but more about how she interacted with them.

Patrick came to mind. The little bit of flirting had replayed over and over in her mind. It had been so unexpected. And pleasant. She could not deny her attraction to him.

She pushed all thoughts of Patrick out of her head and turned her attention to the problem with the property. She supposed she could stay on for a couple more weeks and see how things turned out in regard to the floor, and also to make sure there were no other surprises in store. Her money wouldn't last forever, but she didn't really have to be home until the end of August. And even though it would cost money to change the date on her airline ticket, she could stay and make sure everything got done. In the end, she decided to stay on for another two weeks.

The folder from OHG on the desk caught her eye, and she picked it up. She got comfortable on the bed and leafed through it again, still not believing their more-than-generous offer. It would solve all her problems. She could sell it to them as is. There was no logical reason why she shouldn't accept their offer. But still, something held her back.

CHAPTER FOURTEEN

*P*atrick would be the first to admit that Caroline Egan was not just another pretty face, especially after the way she stepped in at the last moment to mind Gemma and Lucy. He knew how she felt about children and yet, she'd offered, and she'd done fine. As he knew she would.

Initially, it had been her looks that attracted him. Those eyes. There was depth in those eyes, and sometimes he felt like he wanted to get lost in them. Something stirred within him that he thought had died with Maureen years ago. He was torn between guilt and the yearning to move on, to make a fresh start. For the first time since Maureen's death, things didn't feel so bleak.

But over the past two weeks, he'd observed Caroline at the bungalow. The woman was not afraid of hard work. There was no task she wouldn't do. And if she didn't know how, she'd figure it out or ask him to show her. All that, coupled with her soft blonde hair and the expressive blue eyes, left him with a longing and desire that was building within him.

But his growing feelings for Caroline were tempered by one indisputable fact: Caroline's life was in the US. She had a future and plans and she'd made no secret of it. She had her own life that was as far away from his as possible.

Patrick's life was in Ireland. It would never be anywhere else. He was tethered there. Willingly. Ireland was his home and that of his daughters and mother and sister. He'd never uproot his girls and make a transatlantic move. They'd already had enough upheaval in their young lives.

The odds were against them and this depressed him—when he let it.

Caroline was leaving the next day, and that was for the best. Patrick had decided to take her up on her offer and take the day off. His mother was coming home from the hospital, and he could spend the day with his girls. He'd make up the time after Caroline had returned to the US.

He pushed all thoughts of Caroline out of his mind. It was time to go to the hospital and bring his mother home. Because this was where his life was.

PATRICK ARRIVED EARLY at the Burke place on Wednesday and was surprised to find Caroline already there. Caroline knelt in front of the fireplace in the front room. In her hand was a brush whose bristles were slick with varnish. The mantel gleamed after the application of a fresh coat of varnish.

"Hey, I can't thank you enough for minding the girls," he said. "You were all they could talk about: Caroline this and Caroline that."

She smiled. "It was no problem at all. Your daughters are lovely. Nice little girls."

She was so pretty, he thought. He scratched the back of his head. "To be honest, I'm surprised to see you here," he said. "I thought you'd be packing. Doesn't your flight leave today?"

She laid the brush carefully across the open can and looked up at him. "That was the plan, but with everything going on with the leak, I've decided to stay two more weeks."

"That's great," he said, meaning it. He hadn't wanted her to leave so her staying longer under any pretense was fine by him.

Caroline looked at the fireplace. "I decided I might as well re-stain this. I sanded it down yesterday."

Patrick couldn't help but laugh. "Do you ever put your feet up?"

"Not really."

But Patrick's joy over her staying on longer was soon tempered by the realization that she'd be around for the wedding the following weekend. A wedding he had told his mother he'd be taking her to, knowing that she wouldn't be around to attend. In his mind, he started to backpedal, trying to figure out how he was going to sort this out.

Caroline regarded him, a small frown line etching her fore-head. "Are you all right?"

"I'm fine," he said. "Just some things on my mind."

She nodded. "I figured it was best I hang around a bit longer, just in case anything else happens with the house."

"Of course. But don't you have to get back to work?" he enquired.

She shook her head. "I work for a nursing agency, so I choose when I work."

"That's convenient."

"It has its advantages and disadvantages," she admitted.

Patrick bit his lip. This was why he told the girls to always tell the truth. It was easier to keep track of. This little white lie to placate his mother and basically get her off his back was now spinning out of control.

"You're not whistling today," she said.

"I'm not?" he asked, distracted. He hadn't realized he did it often enough for her to notice.

"No, it's very quiet from your end. It's like someone accidentally pressed your mute button," she said with a laugh.

He rubbed the back of his neck. "I've got a lot on my mind." He looked at her and wondered if she would go to the wedding with him. But to ask would require courage.

"I'd better get back to work," Patrick said.

FOR THE REST of the morning, Patrick stayed in one of the bedrooms, painting the walls with a roller brush, trying to sort out in his head what to do about the wedding and Caroline. Finally, sighing in frustration, he decided to ask her to accompany him once and for all. He set the roller brush down on the paint pan before he changed his mind or lost his nerve.

Caroline had remained in the front room, finishing up the staining project.

When he appeared in the doorframe, Caroline looked over at him and smiled. He wished she wouldn't do that. She had a lovely smile.

"Everything all right?" she asked, sounding uncertain.

"Yeah, it's fine," he said. "Actually, I was hoping to talk to you about something."

"All right," she replied. She stood up and wiped off her hands on a towel.

"This is awkward," he started with a short laugh. He coughed, his face reddening.

He did not miss the look of apprehension on her face.

"I don't know where to start," he said.

Her smile disappeared and she regarded him evenly. "It's best to start at the beginning."

"That's actually good advice."

"Go ahead," she prompted. Her voice was soft and for a minute, Patrick imagined what it would sound like in the dark.

"It's complicated," he said.

"Start at the beginning," she said again.

"Right. My mother has decided to make it her life's mission to find me a new partner."

"Okay," Caroline said slowly.

"She means well, but if and when I decide on that, I'd like to choose for myself who I want, rather than having someone picked out for me."

"That makes sense."

"She has this idea that if I would just marry our neighbor, Edel, all my problems would be sorted. I've known Edel all my life. Her brother is a good friend of mine."

"But you don't have those types of feelings toward Edel," Caroline guessed.

"Exactly. We have this family wedding next weekend, and Mam went and told Edel that she could be my plus one," he explained.

Caroline said nothing, waiting.

"Edel is a lovely person, and the last thing I want is for her to get hurt or for my mother to get her hopes up."

"I'm still with you," Caroline said. "It sounds pretty straight-forward."

"Here comes the tricky part." He exhaled and spoke quickly, the words tumbling out in a rush. "I told my mother that I couldn't take Edel to the wedding because I'd already asked you and you were going with me. To the wedding, that is."

Caroline blinked several times, surprise and confusion registering on her face.

He spoke hurriedly. "This was when I thought you were leaving. It seemed like a harmless little white lie at the time. You'd be back in the States, and I'd have a reason to give my mother as to why you weren't going."

She leveled her gaze at him. Her expression was unreadable. "And what is it you want me to do?"

He put his hands on his hips, looked down at the floor, and sighed. "I'm sorry for sticking you into this mess." He paused and looked up at her. "Will you go with me to this wedding?"

Her mouth opened and then closed. She looked away and then looked back at him.

Patrick felt his face go scarlet. Why did he feel like he was back in secondary school trying to get up the courage to ask his crush to the debs? "Look, forget I ever said anything. Again, sorry to dump you into my family dynamics." He began to walk away, feeling his face burning.

"I-I-I'll go with you," she said from behind him.

Slowly, he turned to face her.Her cheeks were tinged with pink. "You will?" he asked.

She nodded and said quietly, "I will."

"That's great," he said.

When Caroline picked up her brush to resume varnishing, Patrick noticed her hand was shaking.

CHAPTER FIFTEEN

*C*aroline turned her attention to the outside of the house now that there wasn't much to be done on the inside until the leak was sorted. She stopped at the garden center in Dingle town to purchase some trays of flowers—petunias, geraniums, and some alyssum—and was back at the house by late morning to start repurposing the vintage milk cans into planters. The ocean below was still and flat with no movement in sight. She'd never seen it this calm. The gray skies had lifted and the sun burned bright. It was going to be a beautiful day.

Caroline went over the events of the previous day for the hundredth time in her head. She'd had a restless night thinking about Patrick's invitation to accompany him to his cousin's wedding.

Was this a date? Or was he just trying to placate his mother? Was he as interested in her as she was in him? She wrestled with all of these things, never arriving at a satisfying answer.

And wasn't it all futile anyway? She'd be going home—three thousand miles away—in two weeks' time. Was it sheer stupidity on her part to start falling for him? Especially when the odds of them getting together were insurmountable?

Her thoughts drifted back to the wedding. She had to admit to feeling a bit of excitement about it. She thought she'd go back to Dingle town later to look for a dress to wear.

Caroline was in the midst of these thoughts when a strange car pulled up in front of the hedge, and she wondered who it could be until she recognized Patrick's mother. Ada Kelly got out of the vehicle with Lucy in tow. She waved and called out, "Caroline!" Lucy skipped and ran along the footpath.

Caroline met them halfway between the front door and the hedge. Ada looked much better than she had the other day. Her color had returned and her expression was relaxed.

"Mrs. Kelly, it's good to see you out and about. How are you feeling?" Caroline asked.

"Much better, thank you." Ada smiled. "Glad to be home. Luckily, it wasn't a clot."

"Patrick told me," Caroline said. "But it's always best to get these things checked out." She looked at Lucy. "How are you, Lucy?"

"I'm good," she said.

"You're the best girl, aren't you?" Ada asked with a proud smile. Lucy nodded.

Caroline thought Gemma and Lucy were lucky to have a grandmother who loved them as Ada did. Caroline remembered her own grandmother, how she had loved her unconditionally and how that had anchored Caroline throughout her life.

"I suppose you're here to see Patrick," Caroline said.

Ada laughed. "Oh no. I see him all the time. I'm here to see you!"

"Oh," Caroline said, unable to hide her surprise.

"I'd like you to come for dinner today at one o'clock," Ada said. "As a way of saying thank you for stepping in and helping out with the girls."

When Caroline went to protest about the dinner, Ada wouldn't hear of it. "I'll have to insist. Besides, you must be so tired of eating in restaurants and out. Wouldn't you like a nice home-cooked meal for a change?"

Caroline couldn't lie. "Actually, that does sound nice."

"Good, then it's all settled," Ada said. "We'll see you at one, Caroline. Come on, Lucy, we need to get home and get the dinner on. Company's coming today." She winked at Caroline, took Lucy by the hand, and headed to her car.

CHAPTER SIXTEEN

*P*atrick thought he'd feel nothing but relief when Caroline agreed to go with him to his cousin's wedding. It was one problem sorted. Instead, he felt as nervous as if he were going on his first date. Nervous and excited. Oddly, he felt young again.

He glanced at his watch, saw that it was lunchtime, and decided to head over to his mother's for dinner.

Caroline called out to him as he was about to exit the house. "Patrick?"

He stopped and turned toward her.

"Are you going to your mother's?" she asked.

"I am. It's lunchtime," he said.

"Can I ride with you? Your mother invited me for dinner," she explained.

"She did?" Patrick asked, feeling a mixture of confusion, apprehension, and surprise.

It must have showed on his face, because Caroline hesitated and asked, "Is that all right? Do you mind?" She spoke quickly. "I mean, I didn't think to run it by you. But I don't have to go if it would make you uncomfortable."

His first instinct was to erase that frown that had appeared on her forehead and put her at ease. He reassured her. "No, I don't mind at all." He paused and added, "Do you?"

"No," Caroline said. "I'm looking forward to a home-cooked meal."

Patrick laughed. "Now that we have that established—that neither one of us minds—let's go get some dinner."

PATRICK FIDGETED with his car keys as he entered his mother's house. He tried whistling but it felt loud and forced, so he gave up. He didn't know what to expect or what his mother had planned. Was it strictly appreciation for what Caroline had done the other day, or was the matchmaker in his mother clambering to get out?

"Ma, we're here," he announced when he entered the kitchen.

Lucy was already seated in her booster chair, and he went over and kissed the top of her head.

Ada stood at the stove, and she turned and smiled at them. "Just in time. Dinner's ready." Ada made eye contact with Caroline, wiped her hands on her apron, and said, "Thank you for coming, Caroline. Again, I just wanted to show my appreciation for all you did for us the other day."

Caroline blushed and smiled. "It was no problem, really."

Patrick let go of the breath he didn't realize he was holding. It was just a thank-you dinner. He could handle that.

"Caroline, you sit next to Patrick," Ada directed. "I'll sit next to Lucy."

Matchmaking it is, then, Patrick thought.

He pulled out the chair for Caroline to sit down, and she bestowed on him a radiant smile that made him want to melt.

He wondered if she realized how lovely she was. If she knew

that hers was a face he wanted to look at every day for the rest of his life.

Ada set a casserole dish of chicken curry with rice in the middle of the table. It was one of his favorite meals. He eyed his mother suspiciously. What was she up to?

They made small talk during dinner, and Lucy entertained them with made up knock-knock jokes.

During the meal, he stole glances at Caroline and thought how at ease she looked sharing a meal with them. Like she'd always been there. Like she fit right in. That was how he saw it, and he wondered if she could ever see it the same way. There was plenty of room in his heart as well as his home and family for her.

By the time his mother served her famous pavlova for dessert, Patrick couldn't remember the last time he'd felt as happy.

CHAPTER SEVENTEEN

*C*aroline checked her appearance several times in the mirror in her room at the B & B. First, she put her hair up. Then she let it down. Then she put it back up. Finally, she left it down. She'd purchased a lovely, summery, floor-length halter dress in Dingle. Glancing out the window, she thought the bride and groom were lucky: the sun was shining brightly and there wasn't a cloud in the sky. There was a gentle knock on her door followed by the voice of Joe.

"Caroline, your fella is here," he said.

My fella.

"I'll be right there," she said. She applied lipstick and checked her reflection one more time in the mirror.

Patrick waited for her in the front hall. At his side were Gemma and Lucy, each one wearing an ivory-colored dress. The satin sash on Gemma's dress was pink, while Lucy's was yellow.

Caroline pulled up short, disappointed. Not for one moment had she considered that the girls would be attending this wedding. All the weddings she'd been to in the States had been followed by adult-only receptions. She realized now she'd been stupid to think that. Of course his girls would be going. He'd said it was a family wedding.

Patrick appeared clean shaven with a fresh, damp, just-showered look. He smelled heavenly. His navy suit added a blueness to his normally gray eyes. Caroline swallowed hard, blinked, and balled her fists to still her racing pulse.

He opened his mouth and then closed it, as if he'd been about to say something but thought better of it.

Caroline said hello to the girls, and Lucy jumped up and down, clapping her hands. "We're going to a party! And you're coming with us!"

"I am." Caroline nodded, smiling. Lucy's exuberance was contagious.

"Your hair is lovely, Gemma," Caroline said about Gemma's French braid.

Gemma gave her a gap-toothed smile.

"Are you ready?" Patrick asked.

Caroline nodded. Patrick held one of his daughters' hands in each of his, and that left Caroline trailing behind them. As he buckled his girls into their car seats, Caroline strapped herself into the front seat, careful not to ruin her newly applied nail polish.

Patrick sat in the driver's seat and looked over at her. "You look nice, Caroline."

"Thanks," she said. She stared straight ahead, quiet, wondering—not for the first time—if this was a good idea. In the backseat, the girls chattered amongst themselves. She stole a glance over at Patrick, who looked the way she felt. Uncertain.

AFTER THE CHURCH, the wedding guests proceeded to a marquee set up in a farmer's field. The white tent took up a good portion of the field. Inside, all the tables and chairs were covered in white linen, and candelabras overflowing with fresh flowers were placed in the center of each table. As Caroline looked around at the sea of expensive dresses with matching hats and fascinators, she felt significantly underdressed. She had assumed that since it was a summer wedding, it might be casual. She wanted to crawl under a table to hide her embarrassment.

She edged over to the back of the tent and tried to be as unassuming as possible.

Patrick appeared at her side with two flutes of champagne and handed her one.

"Thanks," she murmured, taking a sip. The champagne tickled the back of her throat.

"Why are you hiding back here?" he asked. His features softened with concern.

"I don't think I'm dressed properly," she whispered. "I didn't know they wore hats to weddings here."

"I think you look beautiful," he said quietly. Patrick reached for her hand, gave it a squeeze, and then dropped it just as quick, surprising her.

"Thank you," she said softly. The one good piece of advice her mother had given her was to always say thank you when given a gift or a compliment. And to never protest, as it was impolite.

They sipped their drinks as the silence stretched out between them.

"Where are the girls?" she asked.

He laughed. "As soon as they saw the other kids, they dumped me and took off."

"Oh, poor you," she said with a laugh over the rim of her champagne flute.

"Let me have a good cry on your shoulder." He laughed, laying his head on her bare shoulder, his smooth cheek warm against her skin. She felt herself go scarlet. Quickly, he lifted his head, coughed, cleared his throat, and said, "Sorry."

"No problem," she said, unable to hide the tremor in her voice. She took a gulp of champagne.

DINNER WASN'T to be served until seven. There was a big bouncy castle with a slide in the field next to the marquee to keep the children occupied, and Gemma and Lucy made the most of it. The children crawled, ran, and jumped all over the playhouse like ants. Caroline stood with Patrick at the end of the slide and kept her eyes on the girls. It was enough for her in that moment to just be with Patrick.

"Gemma and Lucy are so different in looks and temperament, it's amazing," Caroline remarked to Patrick.

"They're like chalk and cheese," Patrick replied.

Caroline smiled. "I haven't heard that phrase before."

"No? It's an Irish saying."

From the top of the slide, Lucy yelled, "Caroline, watch me!"

Caroline nodded and stepped forward. She folded her arms across her chest and waited for Lucy to arrive at the bottom of the slide. Lucy landed with her hair flying behind her and lifted her arms up to Caroline.

Caroline panicked and looked over to Patrick, who was deep in conversation with another wedding guest. Unsure, Caroline bent down and reached for Lucy, who jumped into her arms.

Lucy smiled and appeared to be studying Caroline's hair. She fingered a loose tendril and said, "You're pretty, and you have the same color hair as me: yellowlicious."

Caroline burst out laughing, and the young girl surprised her by throwing her arms around her neck and hugging her.

AFTER THE MEAL, Patrick took Lucy to the restroom, leaving Caroline alone with Gemma. The effects of the long day were beginning to show on the young girl. Her arms were folded on the table and she laid her head on them. One of her barrettes clung loosely to a few strands of her hair, and the bow of her sash was slowly unraveling. Gemma's eyes darted back and forth between the guests passing by their table and those on the dance floor.

"Is this your first wedding, Gemma?" Caroline asked. She had no idea what to talk to a six-year-old about. She supposed she should just keep it simple.

The young girl looked at her and nodded.

"Do you like it?"

Gemma nodded again and yawned. "I like all the dresses."

"Me, too," Caroline agreed.

"The pink ones are pretty," Gemma said.

"They are," Caroline said. "Do you have a favorite one?"

The girl scanned the inside of the tent and the dance floor. "That one, over there."

"The girl with the black hair, wearing the pink dress with the flowers on it and the poufy skirt?" Caroline asked, referring to a young woman on the dance floor whose dress swirled with every move she made. When Gemma smiled, Caroline nodded in agreement, "That's a great dress. I like it, too."

Patrick reappeared at the table with Lucy in his arms, sound asleep. "I'm going to take the girls home. It's getting late."

"Sure," Caroline said. She began to gather her things when Patrick's sister and mother appeared at the table.

"Deirdre and I will take the girls back to our house for the night, so you can stay and enjoy the night, Patrick," Ada said.

"That's not necessary," Patrick protested as Deirdre took a sleeping Lucy from him.

Deirdre glanced over at Caroline and said, "Yes, it is."

Caroline reddened.

"Gemma asked earlier if she could have a sleepover, and I said of course she could," Ada explained.

"You rogue," Patrick said to Gemma with a laugh.

Gemma giggled and stood next to her gran, who wrapped her arm around her and leaned into her. "You're my girl, aren't you?"

Gemma nodded.

"Ready, Ma?" Deirdre asked. She looked at Patrick and Caroline. "Enjoy the rest of the evening."

"Thank you."

"Say goodnight to your daddy," Ada prompted.

Gemma hugged her father and turned toward Caroline, surprising her when she hugged her, too. Caroline closed her eyes, touched.

After they departed, Caroline said, "You have a lovely family, Patrick."

"Thank you," he said. "I don't know how I would have coped without them when Maureen died. It's because of Ma and Deirdre that I can work and provide for my girls." Patrick pulled his chair closer to Caroline's.

"I envy you that, having someone who has your back," Caroline said.

The lights dimmed in the tent until only the fairy lights that were strung around the tent glowed, giving the space an ethereal feel. A slow song drifted out from the speakers.

Patrick stood up and held out his hand. "Will you dance with me, Caroline?"

Without hesitation, she stood up and laid her hand in his, hoping he wouldn't notice that she was shaking.

On the dance floor, he pulled her close to him, and every nerve ending in her body went on high alert. Her heart thrummed when he placed his hand on the small of her back.

She could hear her own pulse in her ears. She couldn't remember the last time she'd felt like this. High school, maybe? When she'd been crushing on some upper classman? She'd thought that part of her life, namely outright desire, was back in her adolescent past. But her body was telling her something else.

At midnight, a long table was set up with tea and coffee, sandwiches, desserts, and wedding cake. Caroline carried two cups of tea back to their table while Patrick carried two plates of sandwiches and cake.

It felt like a date to Caroline as they sat there, drinking tea, eating slices of wedding cake, and leaning into one another, whispering. When they finished, Patrick said, "Let's dance some more."

She went with him back out to the dance floor, happy to be in his arms once again. He smelled so good: like sandalwood and cedar, and she loved the way she felt in his arms. How he seemed built for her. The longer they stayed on the dance floor, the closer Patrick pulled Caroline to him. Their bodies molded into one another as if they were each one half of the same mold.

After three dances, Caroline pulled back and announced, "I need some air."

He gave her hand a gentle squeeze and led her off the dance floor, heading toward the exit. Outside, the night air was chilly, and she rubbed her arms. Gallantly, he removed his jacket and draped it over her shoulders.

"Thank you," she said.

Despite the nip in the air, the evening was beautiful. The sky was inky, with a vast expanse of twinkling stars.

Caroline stood next to Patrick, unable to take her eyes off him. She tried to memorize every detail about his face: the shape of his eyes and the fine lines around them, the set of his mouth, the planes and angles. She could hear the surf somewhere in the background. It seemed no matter where she went on this peninsula, she could always hear the surf. And that relaxed her to no end.

Her stomach fluttered as Patrick turned to face her. His eyes met hers and his gaze drifted slowly to her lips. The hair along her arms raised, and goose bumps erupted. He leaned into her and lowered his voice. "Caroline . . ."

Caroline searched his face, anxious to close the distance between them. It seemed as if he were on the other side of the world. Hesitantly, she reached up, her hand trembling, and touched the side of his face. His lips came down softly on hers and she closed her eyes. He slid his hands around her waist and pulled her closer to him. Her body ignited under his touch and her knees weakened. He kissed her, soft and slow at first. Hesitant. Cautious. Like dipping your foot in the water to test the temperature. As his confidence grew, his kiss became more insistent. His hands roamed up along her arms and rested on the sides of her face. She relaxed with the feel of his rough hands on her skin. She could feel every callous of his workman's hands. She pulled him tighter to her, her hands running up and down his back. He kissed her hungrily, like a parched man given a glass of water. And she matched his kiss with a ferocity of her own.

Abruptly, he pulled away, clenching his fists, and muttered, "I'm so sorry, Caroline. I can't do this."

Caroline stepped back, breathless, her head spinning. She knew she was flushed and it embarrassed her.

"Do what?" she asked, afraid of the answer.

He regarded her with a pained expression. Unclenching his fists, he waved his hand around. "This. Us."

Her chest tightened, causing her physical discomfort. She wasn't going to have another man reject her. Not again.

Her body went rigid and she crossed her arms over her chest. "It was just a kiss. Don't read too much into it. It wasn't a marriage proposal or anything," she said tightly.

His head snapped back and he regarded her for a minute. "Right, then."

"It's late. We should go," she said.

Before he could see the tears that had welled up in her eyes, she turned away from him and marched back to the marquee. She pulled his coat closer around her, breathing in his smell.

It hadn't been just a kiss to her. It had been everything.

CHAPTER EIGHTEEN

*P*atrick was never so grateful for anything as he was for the presence of Charley the plumber at the Burke place. It meant he and Caroline did not have to talk about what had happened. Not the dancing. And definitely not the kiss. The only problem was, it had been all he'd thought about since the wedding.

He remembered how he'd pulled her into his arms on the dance floor. How her curves fit perfectly against his own body. How outside, feeling emboldened by the night air and how lovely she'd looked, he'd leaned into her. He'd wanted to kiss her for a long time. It was something he'd imagined. Then it was as if the urge had become too great. When he'd given in to that temptation and laid a kiss on her lips, he'd felt something he hadn't felt in a long time: whole. But fear had overwhelmed him, causing him to pull away abruptly. The wounded look on her face still haunted him.

All week, she'd given him the silent treatment. He wanted to talk to her, to tell her about his confusion. How he was attracted to her. How he desired her. And how those feelings overwhelmed him. He knew she was someone he could talk to. Confide in. But that would require courage, to admit to feelings that were both unexpected and terrifying. His fears about the geographical distance between them and the fact that he had his two young children to consider stopped him from seeking her out.

Because things were so non-verbal between him and Caroline, the booming voice of the plumber sounded even louder than usual. The noise from his Kango hammer as he busted up the floor in the kitchen was a godsend. Patrick couldn't think with all that explosive noise and the house vibrating, which meant he didn't have to think about Caroline and how he felt about her. He went about hanging the rest of the doors, staying as far away from Caroline as possible.

While he'd been busy inside, Caroline had emptied the shed of its contents, throwing most of it into the skip, but reclaiming a few pieces. The two old milk cans had been scrubbed clean and planted with red geraniums and purple petunias, and now flanked the front door. There was an antique bike that she'd washed, spray painted red and leaned against the side of the house, filling the front basket with more flowers. She'd taken the milking stool, sanded it down, and restained it. It now was in the hall, near the door. Patrick couldn't understand why she was putting her own stamp on the place if she was planning on selling it.

Charley interrupted Patrick and said, "Would you come take a look at this."

Patrick followed him back to the kitchen, and his eyeline followed the plumber's finger to the floor. In front of the hearth, the old linoleum had been lifted, and beneath it was a four-foot by four-foot piece of flagstone.

"Am I removing this? Breaking it up?" the plumber asked.

"Let's ask the boss," Patrick said.

Patrick called Caroline in, and they showed her the flagstone Charlie had unearthed.

"Is it original to the house?" she asked.

"If it isn't, it definitely has been here for generations," Patrick said.

"They probably brought it down from the old quarry," Charley said, referring to a quarry that had been closed for decades. He scratched his forehead. "It weighs a ton, and they would have brought it down the hill by horse and cart and then somehow managed to get it into the house."

Caroline knelt down and rubbed her hand along a two-inch strip of adhesive glue from the linoleum that had covered it.

Patrick crossed his arms over his chest. "Whoever laid the lino wasn't mindful of the flagstone."

"It's not a problem," Caroline said, standing up. "I'll find a way to remove it without harming the flagstone."

"You want me to leave it in place, then?" Charley asked.

"Yes, please," she said. "This is part of the house's heritage."

"That's fine, just so I know. I'll have the trench dug and the pipes finished by the end of the week," he said.

"That's great, because I'm flying home," Caroline said. She did not look at Patrick. "If you run into any further problems, either you or Patrick can contact the auctioneer, Mick Corbett."

"Very good," Charley said.

Caroline walked past Patrick, gave him a quick glance, and looked away. He wanted to reach out and pull her to him, but he resisted.

Patrick followed her out of the house, toward the skip. He stood with his hands on his hips and stared at the ground, chewing the inside of his cheek. She was going home. And she hadn't even bothered to tell him.

"Were you going to tell me you were leaving?" he started.

"I just did," she said, blowing a wisp of hair out of her eyes.

"If I hadn't been standing there, would you have told me or would you have waited until you were running for your plane?"

"Don't be childish," she chided.

His temper flared. "You're angry at me, so you're playing games now. You're mad because I kissed you and pulled away."

Her face turned scarlet, and she didn't answer right away.

"Come on, Caroline, we're grown adults. Consenting adults," he added. "We're not back in the yard at the national school."

"What is it exactly that you want from me, Patrick?" she asked.

Exasperated, he blew out a heavy sigh and lowered his voice. "I don't want you to be angry," he admitted.

"Not be angry? How can I not be? You kiss me and then push me away and reject me?"

He was alarmed. Reject her? How could she possibly think that? "I did not reject you. And if you saw it as that, I am truly sorry, but that wasn't how it was. You're the first woman I've kissed since Maureen died, and it was everything I'd imagined it to be and so much more. But I got scared. I don't know if I'm ready."

"That's fine, I'm going home anyway," she said, walking away from him, indicating the conversation was over.

PATRICK WAS up early the day of Caroline's scheduled departure. He'd asked Deidre to come down and mind the girls. She knew he wasn't going windsurfing. He'd yet to replace his board. Deirdre didn't pry and when he left, he thanked her.

There was one stop he had to make first. There was a small cemetery along the Castlemaine road, a graveyard filled with locals, and he parked his car on the road before opening the stiff gate and stepping inside. Some of the headstones were worn with time, their engravings no longer readable, eroded from exposure to the weather, the names forgotten. Maureen's grave was in the newer part of the cemetery, where there were only twenty or so resting places. He stood for a long time at his wife's grave, studying her name and thinking about her wonderful life, encapsulated within the brackets of her birth and death. Memories flooded him, good and bad. Patrick realized it was time to close the door on this chapter. It would be a part of him for the rest of his life; it would never leave him. But it was time to go forward. He knelt down and touched the grass that had grown over Maureen's grave.

"It's time for me to move on, Maureen," he whispered. "With your blessing, I hope."

After a while, he stood up to leave. When he left, he didn't look back.

If there was one thing Patrick had learned with his wife's death, it was to never leave things unsaid. To not take for granted the person beside you. But most of all, to tell them every chance you had how important they were to you. You could never say "I love you," enough.

It was these thoughts that drove Patrick to Caroline's B & B that morning. It didn't bother him that he might make a fool of himself. That she might reject him. He had lost nearly everything once before in his life. And although Caroline might still leave, she would at least know how he felt about her.

Caroline did not hide her surprise when she appeared in the doorway after Breda had called her. She closed the door of the B & B behind her and stepped outside. A light mist swirled around them.

"I want to talk to you before you leave," he said, his hands in his pockets.

"If you need anything while I'm gone, you can contact Mick Corbett," she said. She crossed her arms over her chest and locked her eyes on his.

"That's not what I mean and you know it," he said. He'd done nothing but think about her and her impending departure.

"What is it then, Patrick?" Her gaze swept from her feet to the view of the beach before settling back on him.

Patrick stepped closer to Caroline, closing the distance between them. He was so close he could smell the perfume she wore. He could see the tiny freckle at the base of her throat.

He didn't know where to start. And her attitude wasn't making it any easier.

"I want you to stay," he said.

"Why?" she asked sharply.

He said softly, "Because I'm falling in love with you."

She looked toward the beach and her expression softened, her eyes wet.

"I'd like you to stay and see where this leads," he repeated.

She swallowed hard and turned back to him. "Do you realize what you're asking me?"

He nodded. "I do. I'm asking you to give up your life back in the States and begin a new life here with me and the girls."

She hesitated. "You're asking a lot."

He nodded. "I am."

She didn't say anything right away. "I wouldn't make a good mother."

"They had a mother. All they'd need from you is someone to set an example and to love them, and if I didn't think you were capable of doing that or becoming an important part of their lives, I wouldn't be here today, asking you to stay."

He could see the uncertainty in her expression, and he pressed on. "But I'm not asking you to stay because of the girls. I'm asking you to stay because of *me*."

Finally, her eyes cleared, her expression went from unwavering to firm, and she said evenly, "I can't. I can't do it. Not even for you. And how I feel about you." After a pause, she added, "Or how I feel about your girls."

He nodded. "Okay. Listen. Go home, get back to your life.

But if you should change your mind and want to take a chance on a bit of happiness, I'll be here."

"You would wait for me?" her voice was incredulous.

"Yeah, I would," he said. He leveled his gaze at her. "Because you're someone worth waiting for."

She didn't say anything for a bit. She simply regarded him as if trying to process what he'd said. Finally, she said, "I've got to get on the road. Pre-boarding and all that." She turned from him, her gaze shifting to the beach.

Patrick said nothing as she went inside, closing the door behind her. Everything he had come to say, he'd said.

A MONTH AFTER CAROLINE LEFT, the work at the bungalow was completed. On the last day, Patrick took one final walk through the place, making sure everything was done and everything turned off. He'd finished filling the skip the previous day with garbage and debris, and the company had picked it up that morning.

He stood in the front window, gazing at the beach, thinking of Caroline. He'd thought of her every day since she'd left.

After a while, he gathered his tools and left, locking the door behind him.

The next day as Patrick drove by, the auctioneer was putting up the "For Sale" sign on the house in the pouring rain.

CHAPTER NINETEEN

aroline walked through the college quad. She didn't see the old trees with their rich colors or hear the footfall through the crisp autumn leaves, or even notice the lingering smell of woodsmoke from the bonfire that had been held in the quad the previous night. She'd just left a meeting with her clinical advisor, and she felt like the weight of the world had been lifted from her shoulders.

She made it to the parking lot, and not long afterward she pulled into her driveway without even remembering the drive home. She sat there for a while, staring at the house. Eventually, she managed to get out of the car and head toward the front door. The porch was covered in fallen leaves, but she ignored them. She picked up the mail from the box, went inside, and threw it on the console table without a glance.

It had been more than three months since Caroline had arrived home from Ireland to find the house looking just as she had left it, but feeling different: the hallways echoing, the fireplaces with Victorian tile surrounds empty and cold, and the house quiet and empty. An appropriate symbol for her personal life. Even after all this time back, the house still felt strange. It no longer felt like home. Who would have thought that she would be so transformed by her trip over the summer that in her own house, she no longer felt at home?

Patrick had not been once out of her mind since she left Ireland. She missed him. More than she thought she would. Their last encounter had played over and over in her mind. She'd lain awake in bed at night, playing the game of what might have been. If ever she'd wanted a do-over in her life, that was it. Why had she run? Why hadn't she worked something out with him? She couldn't look at a banana without thinking of Lucy. She couldn't see a fancy dress without Gemma coming to mind.

Because she'd felt it would never work. How could it? Could she really be expected to turn her back on her life in America? All that she held near and dear? But then really, what was so near and dear? She'd no family, and the few close friends she had, had families and lives of their own. She had her career, but was that really all there was? One thing she'd learned at hospice was that no one on their deathbed ever wished they'd spent more time at work. At the end of life, it was all about people and relationships, no matter what form they took. She sighed and collapsed on the sofa.

The house was unnaturally quiet. How had she not noticed that before? The loudness of the silence unnerved her. Usually, she loved the quiet. Golden, autumnal sunlight streamed through the front windows, the hardwood floor shining beneath it. She walked through the house, the floor creaking in its usual places. Looking around, she thought about her past and more specifically, her past with Kevin. As much as she loved this house—after all, she had put her heart and soul into it—it remained a symbol of her relationship with Kevin. A relationship that was no more. She headed out the front door, bypassed the expensive white wicker rockers, and sat on the front steps. She was more than ready to move on from Kevin. And the house. She just hadn't known it until she'd come home. She fingered one of the blooms of the chrysanthemum in a pot on the top step.

Patrick came to mind. Beautiful Patrick. She hadn't known it was possible to feel that way about another human being. It defied logic. Insta-love was not how she operated. She was a planner and a preparer. She mulled things over and thought them through carefully. She didn't do anything or make any decisions without having a proper think. Shouldn't you get to know a person over time? Develop a friendship first?

She leaned forward and put her head into her hands. A life most different than the one she had expected was waiting for her three thousand miles away. Her own life felt flat in comparison, and nothing interested her. When she'd first come home, she'd thought it was just your typical post-vacation blues, but it hadn't let up. When she'd gone to orientation at the college, she'd found she just wasn't feeling it. Walking around the campus and going to the bookstore should have left her with some degree of excitement. But it didn't. And that was a revelation that had shocked her. It didn't take long to come to the sobering realization that she wasn't going to be pursuing her nurse practitioner degree after all. So that day, she'd done the only thing she was sure of: she met with her clinical advisor and then marched to the registrar's office and resigned from the college, withdrawing from all her classes.

She'd decided she wanted to live in the house in Inch. She'd seen the pictures the auctioneer had put up online and had fallen in love with the place all over again. She'd refused OHG's generous offer, and then she'd refused any subsequent offers the auctioneer had put to her. She just couldn't sell it. It was her home and hers alone. Looking back, she could see that Maeve Burke had known what Caroline needed all along: a home to call her very own.

Caroline realized that although her past had been here in the United States, any future—any kind of happiness—was across the

Atlantic, in Ireland. In her wildest dreams, she would never have considered moving to a foreign country for love. But there she was.

The beautiful thing about nursing was that you could work anywhere. She was going to apply for Irish citizenship based on the fact that her grandfather, who had died before she was born, had been born in Cork.

Mentally, she began to prepare a list of all the things she'd need to do before her big move. In her mind, she went through each room, deciding which pieces of furniture she would take with her. Calling an international mover was the first thing she'd do in the morning.

A tear slipped down her cheek. She hugged her knees close to her body, smiling. Excitement propelled through her. A new dream was taking shape.

There was a home in Ireland waiting for her. But more importantly, there was a man who loved and wanted her. She'd be the first to admit that taking on the responsibility of his children terrified her. But he was offering something she'd never considered before: a family of her own.

America might have been her home, her heritage, and her past, but Ireland and Patrick and Gemma and Lucy were definitely her future.

CHAPTER TWENTY

The arrival of autumn in Inch saw the disappearance of the sun and the emergence of dull, gray, raining skies. The heat and bright sunshine soon became a distant memory. To Patrick, it seemed as if Caroline had taken the sunshine with her when she'd returned to the States months ago.

On the second Monday in October, Patrick shivered as he pulled on his winter wetsuit. A light mist fell around him. He'd picked up a secondhand windsurfing board via the surfer guy from the caravan, and it had allowed him to distract himself from the void in his life. Namely Caroline. The used board would do until he could afford a new one. Maybe next year.

From where he zigzagged across the water, he could just make out the roofline of his own home and below that, Caroline's bungalow. He could not see the "For sale" sign that still hung there. He'd heard from Mick Corbett that Caroline had received a few offers and had refused every one of them, including the one from OHG. He couldn't understand why she hadn't sold it. She'd made it clear that she wanted to unload it and get on with her life back in the States.

The waves were choppy and fierce, and the board tried to tug itself out of his control, but years of experience came to his aid. It felt good to struggle against the wind to keep the board and himself upright. Exhilarating was the word. After an hour, exhausted, he pulled his board and sail out of the water and, breathless, carried it underneath his arm as he trudged through the icy water to the shore. At his car, he stripped off the wetsuit and towel dried quickly, trying to ignore the brisk wind. Once dressed, he glanced up and surveyed the rest of the beach. There was a lone woman walking on the beach, toward him. He opened his car door but something made him look up again. His mouth fell open in surprise.

"Hello, Patrick," Caroline said with a smile. She was all wrapped up in a heavy coat and scarf. Her blonde hair peeked out from beneath a navy knit cap and her blue eyes blazed brightly amidst all the gray.

"Caroline!" he said, his voice breaking. All the cracks and broken parts began to fill up with something he'd long given up on: hope.

"Does your offer still stand?" She asked, smiling and stepped closer to him.

His heart thundered. "It will never expire," he said.

"Whew," she joked. "I'm glad to hear that. Because I've just moved here. I'm going to live in Maeve Burke's house."

"Your house," he corrected, smiling, thinking of all the promise this turn of events held for him.

She stomped her feet against the damp, looked down, and repeated, "My house."

"May I kiss you?" he asked, searching her face.

"I hope so!" she said.

Patrick took Caroline in his arms and whispered, "Welcome home, Caroline Egan."

EPILOGUE

 *ive Years Later . . .*

CAROLINE LAY in her hospital bed in Tralee General Hospital. She was expecting Patrick and the girls soon. She had good news for them. She was being discharged that day instead of the next. She'd been in for a partial hysterectomy, and she needed to get home if only to prove to Patrick that she was all right. He'd been anxious ever since she'd gotten her surgery date. Caroline knew it was because of what had happened to Maureen, and she was sympathetic. She'd be out of work for about eight weeks, recovering. And although she'd spent her whole adult life working full time, she was looking forward to being a stay-at-home mom for those weeks.

She heard someone in the doorway and looked up to see Patrick's mother there.

"Ada!" Caroline said.

Patrick's mother smiled and walked into the room, her handbag on her arm.

"How are you feeling, Caroline?" she asked.

"I'm fine. I'm going home today," Caroline told her.

"Oh good. Patrick and the girls will be delighted. I had them for dinner yesterday, and the three of them are lost without you." She laughed. "Anyway, that's great that you'll be coming home. Why don't you come for dinner tomorrow? You're not going to want to cook."

"That would be lovely, Ada," Caroline said.

They chatted for about twenty minutes about some of the locals and gardening. Once Caroline had started working as a public health nurse in the area, she'd grown to know almost as many people as Ada did. Now when Ada spoke about the local people, Caroline knew who she was talking about. When Caroline had married Patrick, Ada had also been helpful and generous with advice regarding Caroline's back garden.

Ada wished her well and departed, reminding Caroline of the dinner planned for the next day. She wasn't gone five minutes when both Gemma and Lucy appeared in the doorframe, hesitant. Gemma held a bouquet of sunflowers, and Lucy had two "Get Well" balloons in her hands. Now eleven and nine, the girls were starting to shoot up in height.

Caroline smiled at them and patted the bed on both sides of her. "Come on, I've missed you."

Lucy ran and jumped onto the bed next to Caroline, causing her to wince. But as the younger girl snuggled up to her, it was soon forgotten. Gemma, always the more thoughtful and cautious of the two, set the flowers on the windowsill, then took the balloons from Lucy and tied them to the hospital bed. Only then did she climb into the bed on the other side of Caroline.

Caroline kissed the tops of the girls' heads. She'd missed them all so much. She'd missed her life. The last few days in the hospital, she'd been bored out of her skull. There were so many things she missed: Pancakes and sausages on Saturday mornings. Game night on Fridays, where Monopoly was the agreed-upon favorite. She'd introduced them to some American things, like macaroni and cheese, and s'mores roasted on the firepit outside. They loved the s'mores so much that once the warm weather was gone and the firepit stored away for the winter, they roasted them over the hearth in the house. There was barbecue on the Fourth of July, where the girls decorated everything in red, white, and blue. And at Easter, they loved baskets full of candy being hidden in the house. She also introduced the concept of pajama days, where they'd lounge around all day in their sleepwear, eat snacks, and watch movies.

Lucy had taken a shine to her stepmother right away, but it had taken Gemma longer to come around. Over a year. As a newbie to parenting, Caroline had decided the best thing to do was to spend some time alone with her. So every Saturday, she and Gemma had spent the afternoon together doing something special. As Gemma got older, just going for a cup of coffee and a sweet was enough. Caroline was already planning to take her for her first manicure and pedicure for her next birthday.

Caroline couldn't love either girl any more if they'd been her own.

"How's Bruno?" Caroline asked after her orange-striped cat. It had been a wedding gift from Patrick when they'd married four years ago down on the beach. Caroline had given him a brand-new board for windsurfing.

"He jumped on Daddy again this morning," Lucy said.

"Oh no," Caroline replied. The cat, for whatever reason, was a top-of-the-cabinet surfer. He paced along the top of the kitchen cabinets, and then he'd dive-bomb—kamikaze style— landing either on Patrick's head or shoulder. This maneuver never failed to startle Patrick, resulting in lots of broken dishes.

Caroline bit her lip. "Anything break?"

"A glass," Gemma replied casually, now used to these regular feline occurrences.

"I thought it was a teacup," Lucy said, frowning.

Gemma shook her chestnut-colored head. "No, it was a juice glass."

"Was Daddy mad?" Caroline asked.

"Not really," Gemma said. "I think he's getting used to it."

"He said the only reason he allows Bruno to stay is because he loves you so much." Lucy laughed.

"Who? Daddy or Bruno?" Caroline grinned.

There was a five-second delay, and then the girls burst out laughing.

Patrick arrived, smiling, and Caroline and the girls started laughing again. Caroline gave him a smile and a wave.

"Girls, you shouldn't be in the bed with Caroline," he said. He leaned over the bed and kissed his wife, lingering for a moment.

The girls looked at him and then back to Caroline.

"Cara said it was okay," Gemma informed him.

After she and Patrick were married, Caroline had not wanted the girls to call her "Mom." She said they had had a mother, and she wasn't there to replace Maureen. One day, Gemma had arrived home from school and announced, "We'll call you 'Cara.'" It was the Irish word for "friend" or "relative." And as it was close to her actual name, Caroline was delighted. And it had stuck.

"They're fine. Leave them be," Caroline said, smiling. "Did the guests arrive?"

After Caroline had returned to Ireland, she'd taken her property off the market and had moved into it while she began her relationship with Patrick. She'd spent the year putting her own stamp of design on the place, and it had become her own home. By the end of that first year, she knew she owed a debt of gratitude to Maeve Burke that she'd never be able to repay. The only thing she could do was to love and appreciate the place. Once they were married, they'd decided to hang on to the property and lease it out via Airbnb.

"Right on time." Patrick smiled. "Nice German couple."

"Cara, maybe we could have a pajama day when you come home," Gemma suggested.

Caroline looked at her stepdaughter. "That's a great idea."

Gemma nodded and snuggled into her.

"We've picked our movies that we're going to watch, and we just have to pick our snacks," Lucy announced.

Patrick laughed. "It sounds like I'll be doing a snack run soon."

"Chocolate!" the three of them said in unison.

"And I have news." Caroline smiled. "I'm going home today instead of tomorrow."

Patrick frowned, confused. "Why?"

She laughed. "Stop worrying. Because I'm doing that well." She pulled the girls closer to her. She looked from one girl to the other. "I just want to go home. I miss my family."

"And your family misses you." Patrick smiled.

"We do!" Lucy piped in. "Daddy's pancakes aren't as nice as yours."

Caroline looked over at her husband and smiled. He shrugged. "I tried. I really tried." Then he added. "You've spoiled them."

She laughed, and joy streamed through her. She loved them all and couldn't wait to go home.

Life was good.

ACKNOWLEDGMENTS

Most written books are not the work solely of the author writing them. There are lots of people who help either directly or indirectly.

First and foremost, to Desmond Byrne of Rusheen Bay Windsurfing, Galway, Ireland for his time and patience in graciously answering my questions about windsurfing. Any mistakes in regards to this topic in the book are mine and mine alone.

Juliette Bahr, who coined the term 'yellowlicious' many years ago and it is just too good a word not to use.

And finally, Inch Beach, the home of my soul here on earth, for inspiring this book.

ALSO BY MICHELE BROUDER

The Escape to Ireland Series

A Match Made in Ireland

Her Fake Irish Husband

The Happy Holiday Series

A Whyte Christmas

This Christmas

A Wish for Christmas

The Happy Holidays Box Set Books 1-3

Soul Saver Series

Claire Daly: Reluctant Soul Saver

Claire Daly: Marked for Collection

Claire Daly: Soul Saver Double Box Set

WEBSITE

If you find any typos or other problems, please let me know. As hard as we try, a few typos always manage to slip through. I'd love to hear from you. Feel free to reach out to me at michele@michelebrouder.com

Visit my website and sign up for my newsletter at www. michelebrouder.com to get exclusive bonus material as well as news about upcoming releases and other fun things. I hate spam just as much as you and you can be assured that your email address will never be passed on to a third party.

Warm Regards,
Michele Brouder

ABOUT THE AUTHOR

Michele Brouder is originally from the Buffalo, New York area. She has lived in the southwest of Ireland since 2006, except for a two-year stint in Florida. She makes her home with her husband, two boys, and a dog named Rover. Her go to place is, was, and will always be the beach. Any beach. Any weather.

Made in the USA
Coppell, TX
25 May 2021